# Evil Side Of Money II

## A novel

By

# Jeff Robertson

RJ Publications, LLC

Newark, New Jersey

D1586022

The characters and events in this book are fictitious. Any resemblance to actual persons, living or dead, is purely coincidental.

RJ Publications
**mtymn19681@comcast.net**
www.rjpublications.com
Copyright © 2008 by Jeff Robertson
All Rights Reserved
ISBN 978-0-9786373-9-2

Printed in Canada

September 2008

1-2-3-4-5-6-7-8-9-10-

## ACKNOWLEDGEMENTS

I would like to first, thank God, for the gift he has given me, and the understanding of the responsibility that has been bestowed upon me to accompany this gift.

I'd like to thank Lela and Richard Robertson for their bond in 1967, which made this all possible.

L. Renee' Robertson for her love and support, you're the genuine article baby!

J'nae, Jayla, and Jazmyn, daddy's babies!

Richard Jeanty for believing in the talent, the project, and me. It's amazing what can happen when brothers help each other!

Thanks to Daveda L. Flute for your work. Keep your head up lil' sis!

Thanks to Ms. Eve, the Lab, and Forilla Records for the MySpace page loved it!

.....And thanks to all who have supported me through this project by reading and encouraging me to live out my dreams, there are too many of you to name individually. May God bless you all.

# CHAPTER 1

## LOVE AND MURDER

**Saturday Morning, Chicago Ridge**

As Detective Jackson parked her vehicle along the road she noticed what she would describe as a circus. There were police squad cars from every agency within a ten-mile radius present.  There were also community activists, a throng of news reporters from all of the local stations, members of the local religious community, politicians, and general onlookers – the scene was a bit chaotic.

"Who's in charge here?" Detective Jackson asked flashing her badge.

"That would be Detective Sergeant Faulkner over there," a policeman replied.

"Detective Faulkner, I am Lieutenant Detective Diane Jackson from area one in Chicago.  I was sent over to help out and get some information about the situation here," Diane said.

"Humph…now you guys come.  Well here's the information Detective.  I got a husband, his wife, their seven-year-old daughter, and a member of their staff…all shot gunned to death on a robbery.  Is that enough information?" Detective Faulkner said angrily.

"Ok…may I see the scene please?" Jackson asked.

"Sure, go right ahead," Faulkner said sarcastically.

As Jackson walked past the various policemen and other law enforcement, she could feel the tension and contempt they had for her.  Some even pointed and whispered.  Jackson took off her jacket and placed on some latex gloves.  Then she walked into the convenience store. The scene was a bloody mess, as people from ballistics and the coroner's office were brushing for prints and taking pictures.  Behind the counter were Thomas Kennebrew and his wife, Becky, both shot in the chest and lying on their backs wearing looks of terror on their faces as death masks.   Upon first noticing them Jackson flinched and closed her eyes briefly in sorrow.   Slumped over the counter was nineteen-year-old Eric Simpson shot in the head, with his pockets turned inside out signifying that someone had taken his money.  In the corner was the most horrific sight.  It appeared to be a little girl shot in the face and neck area, but because of all the blood, Detective Jackson wasn't sure.  She had been lying on top of a teddy bear.   The sight made Detective Jackson walk away in tears.

"Yeah, that was my first reaction, too.  That's their daughter, Elizabeth.  She was a sweet little girl who always hung out here with her parents.  It's a damn shame.  I am Sergeant Sanders with Chicago Ridge and you are?"  the man said.

"I'm sorry.....I am Detective Jackson from area one in Chicago," Jackson said between sobs.

"Good to meet you...uh do you have anything? Any leads at all for us?" Sanders asked.

"I was hoping *you* all had something that *I* could use," Jackson replied.

"Just the kid over there...he's the one that discovered the bodies this morning.  He says he was coming in for work and the lights were on and the door was opened," Sanders said.

"Can I talk to him?" Jackson asked.

"Be my guest," Sanders said.

Jackson felt sorry for the kid. As she walked toward him he seemed grief stricken and extremely nervous.

"Hello, my name is Detective Jackson and you are?" Jackson said.

"Perry…David Perry and I didn't do nothing…..I," the young man said nervously.

"No one said you did anything David. We just want to ask you some questions, that's all. Are you ok with that? May I ask you some questions?" Jackson asked.

"Uh-huh," he replied just as nervously.

"How long have you worked here?" Jackson asked.

"Just a month…I was on the night shift, but Mr. Kennebrew said I could switch over to days because he was thinking about just closing the place after midnight," he said.

"Did you like Mr. Kennebrew?" Jackson asked.

"Yeah, he gave me a job. You see I just got out of the county jail and nobody would let me work. My parole officer pulled some strings and got me work with Mr. Kennebrew. He and I got along well. He was always nice to me and I was nice to him. I didn't have nothin' against him," Perry said.

"David what were you in jail for, may I ask?" Jackson said.

"Well, it was armed robbery, but I didn't do nothing this time, honest. I really liked Mr. Kennebrew and his wife. I would never do anything to hurt them or their little girl!" Perry said standing up excitely.

Detective Jackson looked long and hard into David Perry's eyes and drew her conclusion.

"Ok David, have a seat I believe you," Jackson said sincerely.

"It don't matter Miss...they done already drew their conclusions," Perry said pointing to the onlookers and police.

"If you are innocent David, what are you worried about?" Jackson asked.

"They gonna stick it on me and when something like this is stuck on a black man, it stays stuck!" Perry said shaking.

"Look, that's not gonna happen David. You stay with the truth and nobody's gonna stick anything on you at all. Look, I want you to take this and call this man. He is a lawyer. Tell him I referred you to him. Call him today David. Here's my card if anything happens or if you remember anything give me a call," Jackson said earnestly.

Jackson walked away thinking. While heading toward the crime seen again, Detective Faulkner approached her.

"What are you doing? Is that all you have to say to him? This guy could very well be the killer or know who the killers are and you just give him a damn card and walk away?" Faulkner said bewildered.

"He's innocent...he doesn't have anything to do with this," Jackson said confidently.

"How do you know that? He just told you that?" Faulkner asked.

"I just know...it's in the eyes. I have been doing this a long time Detective. I know when a criminal is lying or withholding something. That kid over there is scared shitless and he's shaking like a leaf. No he's innocent," Jackson restated confidently. As Detective Faulkner went on and on, Jackson noticed something of importance across the room and excused herself from Faulkner. "What's this?" Jackson asked a policeman who was dusting for prints.

"Shoe print. We found it not long after we got here…it belongs to the wife," the policeman said.

Jackson walked over to the dead wife's body and lifted her foot up. The tracks from the dead woman did not match the bloody print by the dead man. Also the bottom of the woman's shoes had no blood.

"Can you get me a mold of that bloody print please?" Jackson asked.

"I guess, what's wrong?" the young cop asked.

"There may have been a grave mistake made here today and I have to make sure that's all." Jackson said thinking.

## Bolivia

As Nate got ready for his "date" with Gabriella, he went on and on about her and how fabulous she was. She was an exotic looking woman and very sexy, but I think Nate was taking it a little too far.

"Man, G, I tell you…this woman is invigorating. I mean she wakes up shit in me I thought never existed. She's definitely the best I have ever been with," Nate said.

"Yeah man, she's cool," I said casually.

"Cool? She's the bomb man. I just hope she digs *me*," Nate said excitedly.

"Oh I think she will. As a matter of fact Nate do you know anything about her? She might be up to anything you know?" I said.

"Yeah I'm gonna ask her some questions tonight…try and see where her head is," Nate explained.

"Good luck and be careful," I cautioned.

"G, the first chance you get, try and snoop around and find out a little more about her if you can. I know we are out of our element, but just try to get what you can," Nate asked.

*What the hell was I going to find out? I mean I knew absolutely no one here! It didn't matter to Nate what I found out; he was sold on this woman. And to be honest I was concerned about that. I guess Nate was right; I am basically a suspicious person.* On my way to meet Jon, I ran into Alonzo near the courtyard.

"Ah G, I have been looking for you. Tell Nate that we will be looking for him to make the drop tonight before you guys leave," Alonzo said.

"No need, we will be staying for a couple more days after all," I explained.

"Oh, want to see more of our country, huh?" he asked.

"Not exactly. Nate wants us to stay because he is on some personal interest," I said coyly.

"Ah a beautiful lady has his interest, huh? Great! Just tell him to be careful. The ladies here love American men. They are all looking to get to the States any way they can!" he said.

The last part of that comment worried me: *any way they can. Was this chick looking to use Nate to get to the States?*

"Hey Gabriella, I'm over here!" Nate said.

"Hey baby, I see you," she replied.

"What do you want to do tonight?" Nate asked.

"Take me dancing!" Gabriella said enthusiastically.

"Well I'm not much of a dancer. Back in the States, I am considered a good stepper," Nate confided.

"Follow me. I will show you how. Over here, we Salsa. Baby, me like to Salsa!" Gabriella said with her Bolivian accent.

"I'll do my best. Look these are a couple of my bodyguards, they are gonna drive us ok?" Nate said.

"We don't need them baby...I want to be with you alone ok?" she asked.

"I don't know. I always travel with my guards back home," Nate said.

"You are not home. Baby, you are with me here in Bolivia. C'mon please?" Gabriella asked.

Nate released his bodyguards and they hopped into the jeep and sped off into the street.

## Chicago Police Headquarters:

"Chief, I need to talk to you. I think I have something on the convenience store murders. You got a minute?" Detective Jackson asked.

"Yeah! Come into my office," Trent resigned.

"I just got back from ballistics and I think we might have something. The bloody footprint near the bodies seems to be that of a woman. The print is small and the tracks on the bottom fit that of a popular women's shoe...I have found out," Detective Jackson exclaimed.

"Is that so? What have you concluded?" Trent asked sarcastically.

"Well Inspector, I think a woman was involved with the killings," Jackson said cautiously.

"A woman? You've got to be kidding me Jackson, because you have a footprint? What makes you think a woman could have committed such a heinous crime like this?" Trent asked.

"Well because of the print and there were small handprints on the counter top. I think that stands for something," Jackson said slightly offended.

"Look Diane you aren't going to get anyone to believe that a woman stormed into a convenience store shotgunned three adults *and* a small child no less. I just don't think it is possible," Trent said.

"Ok. How do you explain the footprint and the small handprints on the counter?" Jackson asked defensively.

"I don't explain them! Maybe the mother struggled and touched the counter before she was shot. Maybe she had on a pair of shoes and changed them later. Maybe someone came in took some stuff and left out. Shit I don't know Jackson, but I don't believe a woman killed these people!" Trent said loudly.

"Why...because of the fact that it is a woman? Maybe that is exactly what the killer wants you to think. You don't have a murder weapon or anything that says it isn't. I think that it's sexist and naïve to think that a woman cannot commit crimes, boss," Jackson said challenging her boss.

"Now look Jack-..." As Trent started his harangue the phone rang. He answered it, had a brief conversation with someone and hung up abruptly. "Well Jackson, you can put that ludicrous theory of yours away. We have the murder weapon now. It was found in an alley not one mile away from the murder scene, along with the spray paint can. Prints were run and they fit exactly to a member of the Gangster Disciples. A petty drug dealer from the west side named Titus Thompson. Looks like we have our man!" Trent said proudly.

Detective Jackson hung her head slightly in defeat.

**Bolivia**

"I have had a wonderful time with you tonight. I didn't know you were such a good dancer," Nate admitted.

"There's a lot you don't know about me chico," Gabriella said.

"Oh yeah? Tell me. Tell me more about you," Nate said inquisitively.

"In time my man…in time," she said coyly.

"No, I want to get to know you. Look I'll tell you about me if you tell me about yourself," Nate said bargaining.

As they sat in the jeep, Gabriella moved closer to Nate and put her head in his lap looking up at the sky.

"I have had a hard life amigo…harder than you can imagine. We grew up very poor and my mamma had to work very hard to feed us – mostly labor jobs," Gabriella admitted.

"What about your father…where is he?" Nate asked.

"He died when I was a baby. Some of the local gangsters kill him because he did not pay tribute. He owned a fruit and flower stand in town, and they kill him," Gabriella said sorrowfully.

"I'm sorry to hear that, you must wish you knew him more, huh?" Nate asked.

"Not really…then I miss him even more," Gabriella said wiping a tear from her eye. "I hate it here baby. It's like if you poor, you no matter. You know?" Gabriella said with her native accent.

"Yeah, but it's beautiful here. Back home it's like a concrete jungle. But here, there are trees, groves of trees, and beautiful flowers and the smell of fruit…it's wonderful," Nate said admiringly. "And the sky, look at the sky. Shit, Gabriella, I can't tell you the last time I looked up at the sky and actually saw stars like that. The sky seems so much clearer here.

Gabriella looked deep into Nate's eyes and rubbed his chest while deep in thought.

"I'm going to miss you so much chico," Gabriella admitted.

"You just met me. You probably have a ton of guys," Nate said.

"You are different chico. You handsome, smart, daring, and a lot of fun," Gabriella said.

"Look Gabriella, do you know what I do for a living? I mean do you really know?" Nate asked.

"I no care...I really like you baby and I know when you leave, I never see you again," Gabriella said.

"Well I'll come back to visit. I got a lot of business with Hugo you know. I'm doing really well and Hugo and I are gonna do even better. I'll come back to see you, you'll see. You think I'm gonna know a fine ass woman like you and never come to see you?" Nate reasoned.

"Baby there are fine women everywhere. You will forget me and soon I will forget you. How you say....out of sight, out of mind?" Gabriella replied.

"I doubt that. I think we have real chemistry. We went dancing, eating, and more dancing, and I loved it. I even......,"

Before Nate could get another word out Gabriella kissed him passionately. Nate grabbed her gently by the hair and began to caress her body. The kiss seemed to last forever in the moonlit night.

"Take me home baby...I want to be with you tonight. I know I never see you again. I want something to remember you," Gabriella said with her passionate accent. Nate couldn't resist. Once they arrived at Hugo's estate Nate carried her to his and G's quarters. Once in the room Nate tossed her on the bed lustfully and began to undress. "You ready for me baby, can you handle me?" Gabriella asked with passion and lust in her eyes. Nate gave a devious smile and ripped his silk shirt off exposing his bare chest and large necklace. Gabriella looked at him with animalistic lust. "Come to me baby. I want you now," she purred. They made love with the perfect mix of lust and passion as the moonlight gave them a romantic setting.

~ · ~ · ~ · ~ · ~

"Man these are some fine-ass broads. You better get one of them, G," Big Mike said.

"Man I'm going to bed...shit I am tired," I said.

"Yeah, but you better take one of these whores with you, you know what I am saying. You remember what Nate said? Hugo set up all of this for us and I ain't about to insult him by turning it down!" Mike said gleefully.

"Whatever man! These bitches could have gonorrhea for all you know. Screw that shit. I ain't taking no chance of catching the clap in Bolivia," I said.

"Yeah, but look at these broads man...they almost built for fucking! Now you can't turn that down. Fuck that I'm going for mine!" Mike asserted.

"Hey G, you grabbing one of these or what?" Jon asked with a statuesque Brazilian woman on his arm.

"I'm straight man, do your thing though," I said. I just didn't trust it. I mean there were beautiful women everywhere, only a few of us and some of Hugo's guys. I just wasn't feeling it. Then Hugo came down.

"Hola everyone! How are you doing?" Hugo asked gleefully.

"Cool. Thanks for setting all of this up for us, we appreciate it," I said. Hugo laughed uncontrollably.

"Thank you...everyone he said thank you! Amigo we do this every night almost. This is not an occasion, it is a way of life here you see," Hugo said mocking me.

I watched as all of the guys drank wine, smoked cigars, and "entertained" the women. There were exotic dancers and prostitutes everywhere. I liked women; I just didn't trust them. I didn't know these women from a can of paint and I was out of my element. It was just a little too risky for me. So I started upstairs to our room. As I inserted the key and turned the lock, I pushed the door, but it would not open. I gave it a harder push and tug, but it wouldn't give way. Then I heard someone starting toward the door. I heard what sounded like a chair being moved from the door.

"Oh, hey G. You back from the party so soon, what's up?" Nate said easing through the door and carefully closing it behind him. He stood there looking like the cat that ate the canary while trying to fasten his black silk robe.

"Aww shit man you got that broad in there I want to get some sleep dude!" I said agitated.

"I know G. Here, go to the room over there. I looked out for you; she had one of the girls clean it up for you real nice. You can get some sleep in there," Nate said handing me a key.

"What the hell Nate? All of my clothes are in there. What am I going to wear tomorrow? And I need my deodorant and shit man. What's up?" I asked.

"G, calm down. I took all of your stuff over there already…your suitcase and all. By the way, did you find out anything about her or what?" Nate asked.

"Not really, I'll holler at you about that in the morning. Besides you fucked her now, what's the point?" I asked.

Nate smiled, gave me the finger, and closed the door. I smiled back and walked away. It was good that Nate looked out for me with the other room. It showed me that he wasn't completely selfish, but with this chick I was worried. I mean Alonzo already told me that most of the women here would do anything to get to the States. And I just knew that's what Gabriella was up to. She saw that Nate was into her and she was playing him. What worried me was if Nate found out that she may have been using him he very well could kill her. I mean if a guy would kill his own father…anything was possible. As I walked out on the veranda I looked up at the sky. There were stars everywhere; the sky was extremely clear; and the moon was full and bright. *What a beautiful country,* I thought. The air was clear and you could hear the sounds of nature all around. This truly was beautiful country, unlike urban America. I began to wonder about what might be happening back home. Dana was hot headed and psycho, there was no telling what we would be going home to. Nate was so tied up with this deal and Gabriella, I doubt if he had even given home a second thought.

Hugo and the guys were wrapping things up. It was five-thirty, the sun was coming up, and I heard the music and revelry winding down downstairs. *Maybe I should have brought one of the women upstairs with me? Nah, the broads were fine, but they seemed just a little skanky for me.* After taking a shower and reading a little, I laid across the bed looking up at the sky through the window once more. Thoughts of my mother and mamma Williams ran across my mind as I drifted off to sleep.

The next couple of days were spent sealing the deal with Hugo. We all came to terms and the first installment was paid. Hugo was as happy as a lark; I believe he really enjoyed us and looked forward to having us as partners. After all he knew there was much money to be made back in the States with the drug trade. All of the guys seemed to love Bolivia, which was cool with me 'cause I knew I wouldn't be back again. I enjoyed myself, but it wasn't a place I wanted to return to anytime soon. Jon was a bit hung over from the previous night's festivities as he knocked on the door.

"Hey G, you got any aspirin up here?" he asked wearing dark shades.

"Hell no man, what's wrong...you sick or something?" I yelled purposely to aggravate him.

"Stop yelling son-of-a-bitch I can hear you!" he lamented. "My head is pounding. I need some aspirin bad."

"Yeah well ring one of Hugo's slaves up here, they'll help you out. And you better get your shit together. We leave today and I need you to set up the terms with Alonzo and Hugo about future payments and stuff," I warned.

"I know man just.....give me a minute or so. Where is Nate at?" Jon asked.

"Shit...still laid up in the bed with Gabriella. I swear, man, the last two days they have been all over town; and back in the bed; all over town and back in the bed; it's nauseating," I said.

"Aww man, let him have his fun. We're leaving today and it will be all over," Jon said.

Just then Mike, Pete, and Fingers came into the room.

"Damn what a place! I could move here tomorrow!" Mike said.

"No shit, I have never had a time like this back home!" Pete agreed.

"Yeah well it's time to wrap it all up now; we've got a plane to catch." I said. As one of Hugo's "people" came in, I heard some talking outside of the window downstairs. I peeked out and saw Nate standing there with a few of the mafia guys loading up the trucks with some of our luggage. "Nate's downstairs guys. We better get all of our shit downstairs now," I ordered.

As we labored down the stairs with our luggage, Jon stopped midway and talked to Alonzo about future exchanges and last minute stuff. As I came out of the entrance and into the courtyard, I saw Gabriella loading luggage on top of one of the trucks.

"Is everything sealed and straight?" I asked Nate.

"Yeah things are cool. Hugo and I came to terms on everything. I will fill you in on the plane," Nate said strangely.

"What is she doing...where is she going?" I asked.

Nate discretely pulled me to the side.

"She's going with us, G. She's going back with us to the States," Nate said a bit above a whisper.

"Nate you can't take that broad back to the States with us. We don't know that bitch or who she represents. For all we know she could be spying on our operation for Hugo!" I said outraged.

"G, relax man...she's cool. It ain't like that; I really dig her and I trust her," Nate said trying to assure me.

"Trust her? Nate you don't even know her! She's just a piece of ass you copped here in Bolivia. Now wake up man and leave this broad where you found her!" I said. Nate looked at me for a second.

"She's going with us and that's it," Nate said as he walked away.

Just then an older woman came running out of one of the side entrances of the house with a servant's uniform on screaming in Spanish. I, as well as the others, assumed her to be Gabriella's mother. They were going at it pretty heavy in Spanish. I guess her mom didn't want her to leave with us. As I glanced up at the house I could see Hugo looking down at the whole scene from a window. This was embarrassing. As Hugo's men started toward us with their rifles in tow, Hugo waved them off from the window. I shook my head in disbelief.

"Nate what the fuck is going on? This shit ain't looking tight at all," Jon whispered loudly.

"Jon did you square everything up with Alonzo and Hugo?" Nate asked.

"Yeah man. Why?" Jon asked.

"That's the shit I need you to worry about. I'll handle this," Nate said.

"What is this shit, G? I know this bitch ain't going with us back home?" Pete asked.

"Hey man, ask your boss. I don't know what is going on. I just want to get back home," I resigned. As Gabriella went back and forth with her mother Alonzo came downstairs toward us in the courtyard. "Alonzo what is this all about?" I asked.

"Well my friend…your brother talked to Hugo this morning about releasing Miss Gabriella to him – seems he is into her and wants to take her back to the States. Of course her mother here doesn't agree," Alonzo said watching the scene.

"Tell me something about this chick Alonzo…what's her background?" I asked. Alonzo pulled me aside and gave me the brief spill on Gabriella. After hearing her history, I shook my head in disbelief. Seems my brother, the chance taker, had fallen for a firecracker and was about to bet the rest of his life on a real longshot.

## CHAPTER 2

## COCAINE AND GABRIELLA

Gabriella Conchita Estivar was born near a vast mountainous range in South America called The Andes to Maria Hernandez and Enrique Estivar in April of 1967. She was the youngest of six children and was a consummate daddy's girl. Her father Enrique was a low level cocaine dealer during the sixties and had children stretched across the Andes. Her mother was a Mexican woman and a laborer until her father's untimely death at the hands of the local drug cartel. The details on her father's death were a bit sketchy, but rumor has it that he took a little money that didn't belong to him. Gabriella had five older brothers who helped their father in the drug trade at the time. When the cartel found out monies were missing, they came after Enrique and the Estivar boys. All of them were murdered and left Maria and fourteen-year-old Gabriella alone. Maria picked up work here and there, working in peoples homes while Gabriella went to school. Soon Gabriella started dating and wound up pregnant. Mother Maria was outraged that Gabriella hadn't held onto her honor. Mother Maria was a proud Catholic woman that had raised her daughter to be a chaste and honorable girl. During the stress of it all Gabriella lost the baby. Mother Maria felt somewhat responsible, so she asked God for forgiveness, and asked Gabriella to work with her in the homes of the well-to-do in Bolivia – which is what brought them to Hugo's compound. Mother Maria was a strict woman and always vowed not to let Gabriella fall for another guy and get pregnant again out of wedlock. But it was 1987 and Gabriella was twenty years old and ready to see the world. Most of the young men around Bolivia were poor and she had had a couple of flings with a few of Hugo's guys, but it never panned out to be much. You see Gabriella was a beautiful girl and she was a vixen – a spitfire of sorts – who knew just how to bewitch a man sexually to get what she wanted. Hugo's guys were just underlings and she was biding her time for an American man with money; Nate happened to be that man. So on the plane I thought I would tell Nate what Alonzo told me about her.

"You got a minute?" I asked Nate. Nate got up from his seat next to Gabriella and joined me about four rows back from her.

"What's up G?" Nate asked.

I let him have it. I told him everything that Alonzo told me about Gabriella and that she was using Nate to get to the States. After the story, Nate just sat there looking at me incredulously.

"What….why are you looking at me like that?" I asked him.

"I'm waiting on you to tell me something I don't know," he said plainly.

"Look G, don't you think I know all of that shit. She told me eighty percent of that already, and I figured out the other twenty. G, I know she wants to get to the States, but I dig her and she digs me. Plus she's green; she don't know shit about American living. I could mold her to my hand. I'm tired of all those gold-digger bitches back home. And I live in constant fear that one of those broads will turn state on us. I'm sick of them asking me for money for their sick momma, their kids, their retarded cousin…I'm sick of it! Plus she's fine; the booty is fabulous; and she understands what we are into. Don't worry G. I can control her…it's cool."

"What about the family Nate? You told them not to get close to anyone. They're out there breaking their necks to abide by your rules; you're gonna look like a hypocrite to them and lose their respect."

"I'm not worried about that shit G. I am the boss and having a relationship with Gabriella is not a threat to our security. And if they have a problem with it, they can go to another country and get them somebody!" Nate said condescendingly.

"You know the guys are talking about this shit don't you?" I asked.

"Yeah, let them talk. Niggas probably just jealous that's all," Nate reasoned.

"They have a legitimate beef Nate. This shit stinks." I warned.

Nate just waved me off and went to the bathroom. *She fit in well with the guys!* I thought as she played cards and laughed and talked with them. They had no problem with her. It was Nate and the blatant way he did all of this that was the problem. Nate told me he talked with Dana shortly before leaving Hugo's compound and she said everything was ok. That was a relief; I was worried about that the whole trip. Jon made a great deal to get us the two hundred pounds per quarter for a pretty good price. The first shipment was to reach the States via boat at the port near Baltimore, Maryland. We had some coast guard guys on payroll to look the other way when it arrived; Jon set it all up. Many of the coast guard guys just wanted in a little piece – you know to keep things quiet. We were to get a call from Hugo's people a week before the stuff set shore giving us enough time to drive to Baltimore with the trucks to pick it up. I wondered who Nate would designate to drive to the east coast to bring the stuff back. It had to be someone responsible; I mean you didn't want some lame getting caught by a state trooper with two-hundred pounds of blow in a truck!

Gabriella worried me, I just couldn't feel right about her coming back with us. I just knew there was some kind of angle. So, I talked to Big Mike.

"Hey Mike, let me talk to you for a minute," I whispered in his ear.

"Cool, what's up?" he replied.

"I don't trust that broad. When we get back to the States, I want you to watch her and I want strict surveillance on her ass you got me?" I said emphatically.

"Hey man you know Nate ain't gonna dig you bugging his female like that," Mike said cautiously.

"Mike just…..please do it, let me worry about Nate," I said slightly agitated. Talking to these guys was like pulling teeth; I mean they had such loyalty to Nate that they were almost robotic!

After about three or four hours everyone in our entourage was asleep including Nate. I looked up and Gabriella was reading a magazine wide awake. So I thought I would go over and pick her brain.

"Hey what's up? I thought you would be sleep," I said sitting in the row next to her.

"Nah. I slept before we got on the plane you know. This is my first time on a plane, I a little nervous," she said in her Bolivian accent.

"Yeah, me too…this turbulence is unbelievable! Look uh, Gabriella you ok? Coming to America? I mean you really don't know any of us that well and with us being in our line of work……," I said feigning concern.

"Oh it's ok…my baby will look after me," she said looking over at Nate sleeping next to her.

"Yeah, but you really don't know him that well either. I mean America is a great place but anything could happen to you over there. How would your family contact you? And I could tell your mother wasn't too happy about you leaving so suddenly either."

"My momma don't want me to grow up...I a woman now. I make my own decisions. She left home at sixteen. I be alright," she said trying to assure me.

"I don't know Gabriella. I don't know if this is a good idea. Also how are you going to deal with immigration?"

"Oh, me and Nate are getting married in a month or so, then I be legal."

"Married!? When did all of this happen? I don't know about this shit. I need to talk to Nate," I said disgusted.

Gabriella looked at me angrily and motioned for me to meet her in the back of the plane. She threw the magazine in the seat as she got up, and hard walked ahead of me to the back of the plane. She was obviously pissed about my comment, but shit, I didn't care. I thought this whole thing was out of control.

"Ok, G what is your problem with me?" she said angrily with her hands on her hips.

"Gabriella, I don't have a problem with you per se, I just think you and Nate......," I said before she cut me off.

"What is this "per se"? What is that bout?!" she said bobbing her head angrily – surprisingly much like a black woman.

"Per se means not really exactly, it means just......," she cut me off again.

"Oh...I not a black woman, huh? I not good enough for Nate, is that it?" she said now visibly angry.

"That has nothing to do with it; that's not what this is about......"

Again she cut me off.

"What's wrong...you a fucking faggot...you want to fuck Nate, huh?"

"What the fuck you say bitch, that's my fucking brother! You new on the block you don't talk that shit to me! You can take your border jumpin' ass back to Columbia, Mexico, Guatemala, or wherever the fuck you're from and-- " I said yelling. Now we were in a full scale shouting match.

"I not Mexican you fucking faggot! You fucking......piece of shit!" she said yelling.

"Bitch, you better go cut some fucking grass or sell some flowers somewhere before I-- " I said yelling.

Just then Nate and a couple of the mafia guys as well as the stewardess came in to see what was going on.

"Hey, hey what the hell is going on back here G?? Nate inquired excitedly and half asleep.

"Hey man you need to get this broad before I knock the shit out of her. She is real out of pocket right now!" I said loudly.

"I not a bitch motherfucker!"

As she said that, she started toward me. Nate grabbed her and picked her up and brought her past me to another side of the plane. She was yelling and screaming, kicking her legs and waving her hands at me like a wild banshee! Jon and Mike walked up and asked what was going on.

"She's crazy, that broad is crazy! I told Nate to leave her ass back in the rain forest somewhere!" I said still angry.

"What were you talking about that got her so mad?" Mike asked. Before I could say anything a stewardess walked up.

"Mr. Williams, you will have to try to keep it quiet. There are people trying to sleep. This behavior is extremely inappropriate," she scolded.

"Did you tell her that?" I snapped back. The stewardess just gave me a disgusted look and walked away. After everything calmed down, I sat down in my seat and ordered a drink to calm me down a bit. After about ten minutes or so, Nate came and sat down beside me.

"G, I'm sorry about that man. She tends to get a little excited and.....,"

"Excited?" I cut him off. "What the fuck? Nate this broad is out of control. I mean right is right. I'm really not feeling this chick man. She's rude, ignorant, and disrespectful, and you need to holler at her about that shit if she's gonna roll with us! But personally I think you should have left her ass back in The Andes some damn where!" I was half drunk by now.

"It's cool man, I talked to her. She knows she was wrong, but I need you to work with me on this G. Just try man," Nate asked diplomatically.

"I'm trying man, I'm trying," I said shaking my head. After a couple more sips of Cognac, I fell asleep. I must have been asleep for awhile when I could feel someone sitting next to me. I opened my eyes and it was Gabriella.

"I sorry G, I just love Nate and I want to fit in with you guys. But you made me mad, like I wasn't good enough for him. Don't you like me?" she asked sheepishly.

"You know Gabriella it's not that, it's just that I don't know you, and I have a hard time trusting people I don't know," I reasoned. "And I'm sorry too, I guess this long-ass plane ride and the stress of this whole trip is fucking with me a little bit," I said apologetically.

"So we have truce?" she said batting her eyes playfully.

"Yeah, I guess. Truce," I said extending my hand. She could be convincing when she wanted, but deep down I still didn't trust her, and she knew it.

"And I promise, I win your trust," she said shaking my hand. I glanced over at Nate and he was looking over at us smiling and nodding his head in approval. Still, I didn't trust her completely.

As we arrived at O'Hare airport, we all were too anxious to get off that plane. It always seems like the return flight is longer than the initial flight. Dana was told to have some mafia guys meet us at the airport with a couple of trucks. As we all walked through the terminal, I noticed that Fingers looked strange, sick even.

"What's up man, you ok?" I asked.

"Nah, I think I got some food poisoning or something. My stomach is killing me," he replied wincing in pain.

"We better get you to a doctor then. Soon as we get settled in I'll have a couple of guys drive you down," I assured him. He just nodded in agreement.

I noticed a newspaper stand and decided to buy a paper. I always like seeing what's been going on in Chicago while we were gone. The news was pretty much what I expected: news about Daley being the new mayor, Michael Jordan and the Bulls, etc. Then a small caption, "Massive Manhunt for Gang Leader," on the front page caught my eye. I quickly opened to the story.

"Hey Nate look at this!" I said excitedly. The story outlined a gruesome killing in the Cicero area naming a gang leader, Titus Thompson, as the number one suspect – in fact the only suspect.

"Well what do you know about this shit, couldn't have happened to a better nigger!" Nate said smiling. The article was pretty short on specifics, just a lot of opinions and accounts of what may have happened. We also read that the FBI was involved with the investigation. "You see G, now when this motherfucker killed Donnell, nobody gave a fuck. Now that some white folk are dead, it's a massive manhunt! This is the very shit I was trying to tell that stupid Detective Jackson bitch. When black people die, it's no big deal; like black lives are worth less than white ones. I hate that motherfucker, but I hope he gets away with it, I hope they never find his ass!"

"Yeah, but would he really be that stupid – to kill a store full of white folks like that? He has to know when they find him he's gonna get the electric chair!" I said.

"I don't think they using the electric chair to execute anymore, G," Mike said.

"Shit, they'll dust that motherfucker's back off if his ass is behind this shit, believe that!" Nate said.

The whole ride home I kept thinking that it didn't make sense. I knew Titus was a dumb gangbanger, but three white people *and* a little girl? It just didn't make sense. Deep within the recesses of my mind I thought he might be getting railroaded.

During the ride back to New Lenox, I noticed that Gabriella was all over Nate, cooing and kissing. Nate was really feeling good since he read the Titus story and now we were back home after just making the deal of a lifetime.

"Hey G, we better talk to our lawyer about Gabriella. She ain't got no visa or nothing. Now she has a waiting period, but we really need to get on that as soon as possible," Mike and Jon warned.

"No need, Nate will probably marry her within the next week or so, watch and see," I said.

"Damn you think so?" Jon asked. I looked at both of them incredulously.

"Watch and see."

As we drove up to the compound we saw Dana, some mafia guys, and some of the domestic help standing outside to greet us.

"I wonder what the hell she has been up to?" I said.

"Don't worry G, it's cool," Nate said chuckling.

As we all got out of our cars Dana walked up to Nate and me and gave us the customary kiss on the cheek for respect.

"What's up boss...how was the trip?" she asked.

"Great, what's up around here?" I asked.

"Same old shit, you know the deal."

"Dana, I told you don't wear those guns out in plain view like that you don't know who could be watching!" Nate said sounding agitated.

"Oh, yeah right," she said flipping her blouse over the huge guns.

"I want a debriefing meeting after we all get cleaned up, in about two hours in the conference room," Nate asserted.

"I'm on it," Mike replied.

Then Gabriella got out of the car bouncing her way toward Dana and placed two bags down at Dana's feet and walked into the house behind Nate.

"Who the fuck is that bitch?" Dana asked.

"That's the new mistress of the household!" Jon said smiling.

"Well somebody better tell that immigrant bitch I ain't the fucking help!" Dana said angrily. I knew right then that Dana and Gabriella would lock horns and that they would never make it in the same household.

"Nate, Jon and Mike suggested we talk to our lawyers about Gabriella; she's not legal and the last thing we need is shit from INS," I warned.

"Way ahead of you brother, I got it all taken cared of," Nate said greeting and playing with his beastly looking dogs.

The house seemed the same. Dana had it smelling pretty good and I immediately went to the refrigerator for a cold American drink. I was sick of all of that Bolivian wine stuff! I looked at all of the stuff we had in the massive stainless steel fridge and decided on a glass of cognac. I walked toward the bar and saw an envelope with some pictures, so I opened it. In it I saw the grizzly photographs of the murder scene which we read about, it made me nauseous. There were even pictures of the little girl with half of her face blown off.

"What are you drinking G?" Pete came in and asked. I quickly stuffed the pictures and the envelope into my inside jacket pocket.

"Oh…just some Cognac, want some?" I offered.

"Nah, you know I am a Gin and juice kind of guy," Pete said proudly. As he walked around me to the inside of the bar to get a glass, I took my jacket off and laid it over my arm, grabbed my glass and started walking out of the room.

"So what do you think…we on our way, huh?" Pete asked starting a conversation.

"I guess, I'm gonna go get cleaned up for this meeting. You know Nate don't like to do nothing late," I said giving an excuse to leave. As I walked upstairs to my room I grabbed my bags and the newspaper and hopped up the staircase taking three stairs at a time. I quickly walked into the room and threw my bags on the bed, took my glass, the envelope and the newspaper into the bathroom and locked the door behind me. I sat on the toilet and looked at the article and the pictures. *How the hell did Dana get these pictures?* The article said the time of death of the victims had to be about 2 a.m. I closed my eyes and started to pray. *Please God, don't let it be what I think it is.* I flipped one of the Polaroids over and made the ghastly discovery. The date read 9-26-87.....2:31am! *That psycho bitch!* I took a long swig from my glass and threw some water over my face to get myself together. I had to tell Nate, before anyone else found out. I put the pictures in my pocket, grabbed the newspaper, and walked out of the bathroom. I heard someone moaning and saw Fingers in the fetal position on my bed with his hands between his legs with tears streaming down his face.

"G.....I need a doctor man......I'm hurtin' bad!" he managed to get out. I called out to some of the mafia guys and we got Fingers down to the foyer. I called for a car to be brought around to the front of the house.

"Get him to a doctor, but make it somewhere in Chicago. Check him in under an alias and call me as soon as you hear something." Turning to Fingers, I said, "Be cool, Fingers, they're gonna take you to the hospital to see what's up, ok? We will be down there later tonight or first thing in the morning," I said comforting him. I checked his pockets for anything incriminating and two mafia guys picked him up and placed him in the car. "Don't tell the people there shit about where we have been or anything, just tell them he came down with something, and remember call me when you hear something," I said loudly. I tapped the hood of the truck and off they went. I looked as they sped off, wondering what could be wrong with him. I would have to figure it out later.  I had more pressing business that needed attention.

I hopped up the staircase headed towards Nate's massive bedroom, but his two beasts were guarding the double French doors.  They were the most monstrous menacing looking animals I have ever seen.  I tried not to show fear; Nate had them professionally trained not to attack me, but I couldn't help it.  They were downright frightening.

"G is that you?" Nate said from inside.

"Yeah, you wanna get me past these beasts?" I asked.

"C'mon in man they won't fuck with you," Nate said laughing.  As I walked past them they both moved to sniff me and once they recognized my scent they sat back down into guarding position.  They gave me the creeps!  I walked through the doors, and Nate was standing in the small room just before you enter his bedroom.

"Gabby's not dressed.  Let's just talk out here," Nate said softly.

"I had to send Fingers to the hospital man, he's pretty sick," I said.

"Sick from what?" Nate asked curiously.

"I don't know…some virus maybe, but I thought I'd let you know that," I said.  Nate nodded in approval.  "You need to know this, too," I said handing him the pictures and the newspaper article that I had circled.  Nate took the pictures, looked at them and let out a soft "damn" that was barely audible.  He studied the article and the pictures rubbing his head in deep thought.  He looked at me, shook his head and closed his eyes.  Then studied the pictures and the paper some more.

"Where the hell did you get these pictures?" he finally asked.

"On the bar downstairs, can you believe it?" I asked.

"Fuck, oh well," Nate said and handed everything back to me.

"That's it, that's all you have!?" I asked in amazement.

"What you want me to do, hold a vigil?" Nate replied.

"Nate this bitch did this. She committed these murders and set Titus up for it and when the police find out….," I said outraged.

"If…if they find out G and keep it down I don't want Gabriella to find out," Nate said.

"Nate do you understand the heat this broad is bringing down on us with this shit?"

"G, I'll address it at the meeting tonight, ok? Now relax. Everything will be alright, you'll see," Nate said trying to reassure me.

"I just want to know when you will stop co-signing for this broad…when we're all in jail?" I said disgusted leaving the room.

Sitting in my room, I started to think about Fingers and his condition when I heard a knock at my door.

"What's up G, got a little info I want you to discuss at the meeting tonight," Jon said. "First I want you to let Nate know that we have to start thinking about opening up some businesses. You know to wash this money a little. Maybe some beauty shops, car washes, convenience stores, whatever. Then I got a little info on a new thing, check this out." Jon handed me a box. As I opened it, I heard some of the mafia guys in front of the house standing around talking and laughing. I looked down and they were playing and talking into what looked like a phone.

"Is this a phone Jon?"

"Yeah...cool, isn't it?  It hasn't hit the hood yet, but I'm telling you it's gonna change everything.  No more payphone shit.  This business is gonna skyrocket here in America, especially in the hood.  Not now, but maybe five to seven years from now," Jon asserted.

"Bigger than pagers?"

"Shit, why would you need a pager when you got one of these?"

"Interesting, who turned you on to these?"

"You know me baby I got connections.  It's my job to stay on top of this shit right?"

"Indeed, good I'll address it tonight.  Good work Jon and tell those guys to put them away.  We haven't made any decisions on them yet," I directed.

"Ok, and G, one more thing.  Maybe we need to start looking into sending a little cash overseas, too.  We don't know how long this shit is gonna last.  I've got some prospects," Jon said leaving the room.

"Ok, I'll look into it.  Any word on Fingers yet?"

"Nothing yet."

"Let me know and don't get high until after the meeting Jon!"

"No problem, I won't," he said smiling back.

At the meeting everything was supposed to be on the level.  We discussed our trip to Bolivia in detail; we discussed the deal that was made.  We then discussed a few minor details and Nate dismissed us all.  All except Dana, he really didn't want to discuss the situation in front of the others.

"Ok Dana, what the fuck happened while we were gone?" Nate asked hesitantly.  Dana told us the whole story:  the fight at the club; the killing of some of the guys involved; the capture of Titus; the convenience store murders; everything.  After grasping everything, I put my head in my hands in disgust. Nate leaned back in his huge leather chair and placed his hands behind his head smiling. "You know Dana that was an ingenious plan, except for a couple of things. First you were instructed not to do anything until you talked to G or myself. Next I instructed all of you to not do a thing to this gangbanging fuck, that I wanted to murder him myself. You kind of fucked that up now, he's on the run. You had better do everything you can to make sure the cops don't ever figure out who committed those murders; and you know in the family, one of the rules is we don't kill kids right?" Nate asked.

"Yeah boss, but I couldn't let her live, she would have identified me, right?" Dana asked.

"Right, but that's still a kid...well fuck it, it's done now. But you better lay low for a while, let the shit die down. Stick around the house and help G out, maybe help Pete get started when that coke gets here ok?"

"Ok Nate I'm sorry I fucked up...won't happen again," Dana said remorsefully.

"That's all I have, what about you G?" Nate asked. I was stunned.

"That's all you have? She goes out there and does some irresponsible shit like that and that's all you have?" I was outraged.

"Yeah, I mean what can we do? She apologized. We just have to make sure the mess stays clean G. There isn't much else we can do," Nate said casually.

"I don't know...say something! Get in her ass or something! She almost sunk the whole damn crew with that shit. It was stupid Nate and ill-advised. How do we know she won't do it again?"

"She said she wouldn't, that's good enough for me." Nate walked over to the mini bar to make a drink.

As he turned his back, Dana stuck her tongue out at me and gave me the finger. So, I gave her one back!

"You know this is some bullshit Nate, but it's cool. I guess when we are all cuffed and on our way to prison it will finally dawn on you how stupid this broad really is!" I said angrily.

"Who the fuck you calling a broad, nigger? Don't fuck with me!" Dana said clearly insulted – which was cool. It was just what I wanted.

"Hey, Hey, Hey…Now let's cool this shit down! I don't want no yelling and cursing in my office unless it's me! Now Dana go. Let me and G talk about this," Nate said. As she walked past me to leave the room she bumped me and called me an asshole under her breath. Once she left the room, Nate sat his glass down and handed me a Cognac. "Sit down G, now look I know you are right. But we need Dana for some future shit I need done. And she is the only one that can handle it for me. Trust me. I will work with Dana and make her understand what she did. But you are absolutely right, what she did was asinine, but you can't just destroy this chick behind that. Trust me G, now we will make sure everything stays quiet and keep her around the house, ok?" Nate said calmly.

"Nate, I hate that bitch…I hate that bitch…I hate that bitch, and by the way I hate that Bitch!" I said loudly. "Whatever the fuck she does from now on Nate is on your head, you're responsible for her ass."

"Wait a minute, you brought her here, remember?" Nate said.

"Yeah, but you're the one that keeps her here. I would've put a bullet in her head long ago." I swallowed the last of my drink and walked out of the room. As I got downstairs Pete walked briskly toward me.

"Fingers has been admitted at the hospital. They said he has a virus or something and they needed to run more tests," Pete said.

"What kind of virus? Did they say?" I asked.

"Shit I don't know... some medical shit. Maybe we should go to the hospital in the morning and check it out, huh?"

"Yeah, let me talk to Nate. Look, go get some more liquor the bar is dry. Take some guys with you."

"Cool got some money?" Pete asked smiling. I reached in my pocket and pulled out about twelve hundred dollars.

"Get what you can and put some cash with that. You drink too! Get good shit Pete, not that generic junk!" I yelled as he walked out of the door. *What kind of virus could Fingers have? I hope he didn't catch anything in Bolivia that we would have to disclose to any doctors,* I wondered.

Nate heard from Hugo and was promised that the first shipment would be delivered in a couple of weeks. We had a code all set up, it was good. Meanwhile we had enough coke to last us until the shipment. Crack cocaine was selling like hotcakes and it would keep us liquid until we got the bulk order from Hugo. We were raking in the big money; we weren't catching any heat from the convenience store murders; and everyone was happy. Except Gabriella was driving everyone crazy! She was taking over the whole damn house!

"Ok G, from now on everyone will eat together in the morning. My Nate says we are a family...we will be a family!" she said with her thick Bolivian accent.

"You know Gabriella we all pretty much do our own thing around here when it comes to eating, besides have you talked to the cooks about all of this?" I asked.

"Yes and she said it will be fine. Everyone will eat breakfast together, like a family." *Yeah,     right. Just try and get everyone at one table eating together, like we were the Brady Bunch or some shit. It would never work!* "Nate do you know about this eating together stuff Gabriella is talking about?" I asked.

"Yeah, I know it's corny G, but it makes her feel needed and like family. It will work you'll see," Nate said reassuring. I wasn't convinced. Later I saw Gabriella all dressed up and walking toward the door.

"Where are you going?" I asked.

"Shopping Derek, would you like anything back?"

"Gabriella, you can't go shopping. We don't do it like that. Now just give one of the guys a list and he will bring back whatever you want," I instructed.

"I am going clothes shopping. They don't know what I like...thank you very much!" She started toward the door again.

"Gabriella, I told you we don't do it like that. We have catalogs. Just pick out what you want and.....," I said as she cut me off.

"My Nate said I can go wherever I want, Mr. G, you no stop me, now excuse me!" She forced her way through and stormed out of the door. I immediately instructed some of Big Mike's guys to follow her.

"What's going on?" Dana asked walking up.

"That fucking broad of Nate's...she is impossible. She doesn't listen. She's pushy as hell!" I said frustrated.

"You don't have to tell me. She's breaking every rule we got here. You and your brother are gonna have to do something about that immigrant bitch before she gets us all locked up!" Dana said.

I hated to admit it, but I agreed with Dana. Gabriella was out of control with her new "rules". She rearranged most of the furniture and had two rooms in the house totally remodeled! She threw away most of the food we had in the cabinets and got all Columbian shit! She changed everything, and the worst part of all was Nate let it all go; he let it all ride. He endorsed the shit. Needless to say people were pissed off! But this time I knew Nate would get at her. This was one of his most sacred rules: no one go shopping and expose themselves too much. I knew he would get in her ass about this one. When he arrived at the house with Jon from one of his meetings he asked about Gabriella.

"Where's Gabby at?"

"Gone shopping," I said.

"Shopping? Who the fuck ok'd that?" Nate asked outraged.

"Shit! She said you did. I wasn't about to get into that!" I said trying to instigate a little.

"Yeah Nate, we thought you ok'd it. G sent some of Mike's guys with her but she's been gone now for about four hours," Dana added.

"Four fucking hours?" Nate asked angrily. He didn't say anything else. He just stormed upstairs and slammed the bedroom door. Then the house phone rang, it was Nate calling from upstairs.

"G let me know when she gets here. Don't say shit to her just call me! And feed the dogs for me!" he said and hug up. He was so pissed he didn't even say goodbye. Dana and I gave each other five because we knew we had her ass now. About two hours later Gabriella put her key in the door and in she walked. The guys had bags and boxes stuffed into about four trucks, as it turned out Gabriella drove to Michigan Ave. downtown and spent nearly sixty-thousand dollars on clothes, shoes, perfumes, and lots of other shit! There were bags from just about every store downtown! The guys were bringing boxes and bags in for about twenty minutes! Then Nate came storming down the stairs. "Where the fuck you been?" he yelled. Dana put her gun in the small of her back and clasped her hands together grinning.

"Oh shit, I been waitin' for this!" Dana said with excitement. I whispered for her to be quiet so we could hear.

"Shopping...I told you I needed some stuff," Gabriella said dryly.

"Didn't G tell you we don't do it like that? You don't just carry your ass out shopping and shit! Gabby, you're gonna follow the fucking rules around here like everybody else, you hear?" Nate yelled.

"Oh fuck you, go to bed!" Gabriella said defiantly. Then Nate slapped her across the face. As she fell to the floor, Nate grabbed her by her hair and began dragging her up the stairs!

"Fucking bitch...when I tell you something you better be found doing it!" Nate yelled. Dana was almost giddy with laughter while the mafia guys kept bringing in the bags and boxes. Gabriella was screaming in Spanish, mixed with English, cursing Nate and kicking while being dragged. "Get your fucking ass in this room, you don't talk that shit to me motherfucker!" Nate was still yelling. One of the guys looked at me to let me know that was all of the stuff.

"Just leave it all there," I said. Nate tossed her in the room past the dogs, and pulled his belt off from around his waist.

"I'm going to teach your fucking ass!" Nate yelled. Then we heard Gabriella.

"Come on black motherfucker, try it!" she screamed.

Dana and I looked at each other surprised. *Was she actually going to try and fight back?* As the dogs lay in front of the bedroom door, we heard screaming and bodies hitting the floor for about a half hour, then silence.

"Go see what they are doing G," Dana said.

"Why me? Shit I don't care," I said.

"Liar, stop bullshitting and go listen!" Dana said. I snuck up the stairs and I could hear Nate and Gabriella going at it hot and heavy sexually. *I'll be damned,* I thought. When I told Dana, she seemed taken aback. "Yeah, he fucking her now, but I bet he make her take all of that shit back tomorrow!" she said emphatically. I agreed.

The next morning I got up pretty early. I had to meet with Mike and Jon and go over the cocaine pick up. Nate was supposed to attend the meeting also.

"Damn, it's ten o'clock, where is Nate at? Is he still sleep?" Jon asked.

"I don't know. He and Gabby got into it last night. I don't know what's up," I replied.

Then Nate opened the office door. He looked terrible. He had on some slacks and a tank top T-shirt, with dark glasses on and scratches all over his neck and shoulders.

"What's up fellas? Let's get started," he said quietly.

"Damn man what the fuck happened to you?" Mike asked. Nate sat down in the leather chair behind his desk, and let out a deep sigh, and rubbed his head.

"Let's just do business Mike, ok?" Nate said. After we adjourned Nate walked over to me and asked me about Fingers. "What's up with our man in Chicago, is he all right?"

"Yeah, he has an intestinal virus...I think we should go see him today. Mike said he can arrange security."

"Cool, while we are in the city maybe we should visit the cemetery...I haven't seen mamma in a while. What do you think?" he asked.

"I'm for it. It has been awhile. You ok, Nate?"

"Yeah, I'm cool. I found out something last night though." he said again quietly.

"What's that?" I asked curiously.

"There's no difference between black women and the Spanish ones!" he said slightly grinning.

"Let's go eat," I said smiling as I threw my arm across his shoulder. When we got to the kitchen, Gabriella was sitting at the table with dark shades on and bruises on her shoulders and arms. Her hair was all over her head, too.

"Good morning G. I'll get all of my stuff out of the foyer in a minute. Had to have coffee," she said just as quietly. Nate walked by her and poured himself a cup. Then Dana came down stairs from her morning workout.

"Damn what did you all do last night – try and kill each other?" she said smiling. No one said anything. Dana got a bowl out of the cabinet and poured some cereal in it and some milk. She sat down next to Gabriella and started eating.

"Aren't you going to at least shower before you eat? You've been working out and you smell," Gabriella said.

"I *smell*? Worry about your ass. I didn't say anything to you sitting at the table all bruised and punched up and shit," Dana said. Then Dana started eating. She wasn't just chewing the food, she was chomping on it. Gabriella looked up at her and Dana had milk coming out of her mouth. Dana looked back at her incredulously and wiped the milk from her mouth with the back of her hand.

"You are so disgusting. You have no manners. Why don't you at least act like a lady?!" Gabriella said disgustingly.

"What?! You don't look so prissy yourself bitch sitting there looking like a fucking prize fighter!" Dana said emphatically.

Gabriella stood up and called Dana some names in Spanish, then Dana jumped up and started yelling at her. I got in between them both and tried to calm them down. Nate didn't say anything. He just took his plate upstairs and closed the door. That's how it was around there for a few weeks: bickering between Nate and Gabriella; and bickering between Gabriella and Dana. Nate and Gabriella would get into a fight and Nate would drag her upstairs. They would punch each other around and then have sex. To say their relationship was tumultuous was an understatement. For the life of me, I couldn't figure out why Nate preferred that kind of relationship above the ones he had with the black women before Gabriella. I guess he was in love, but Dana certainly had no love for Gabriella.

"Look at this shit G. I thought you said this bitch was from the jungle. Look…Prada, Coach, Versace, Vera Wang, how does this broad know about all of these designers? I've been here all of my life and I have never heard of some of these!"

"I don't know Dana, and I don't care. Could you help Mike get security together for our visit to Fingers tomorrow, please?" I asked. As I stood looking out of the massive bay window, I could see it was hazy outside and most likely very hot – unusually hot for the month of May. I knew we were taking a chance hauling Nate into the city, even to see Fingers. Nate was a wanted man all around the city and there was a fifty-thousand dollar mark on his head from the Gangster Disciples, so security had to be tight. While thinking about security, I see a car driving toward the main entrance with some of our black SUV mafia trucks behind it. As it got closer I could see that the car was a pearl-white Bentley with huge chrome rims along with personalized license plates that read MOTH (Mistress of the House). *Oh shit! This broad has went out and bought a three-hundred thousand dollar car!* I could see Jon sitting on the passenger side looking like a sucker! *She must have gotten Jon to sign for it and get all of the legal stuff in order.* I made up my mind that I wasn't going to say or do anything. I was going to let Nate handle it all. But the question was could Nate handle it? Between Dana and Gabriella they were gonna drive the poor man crazy! Sure enough when Nate got home there was a lot of screaming and fighting, then hot sex, but Gabby kept the car.

The next day we were going to see Fingers. Mike had arranged security so tight, you would have thought a diplomat was in town. There were six mafia cars, and one SUV containing Nate, Jon, Dana, and Pete. Nate made me ride with one of the bodyguards in case something went wrong. When we got to the hospital in Englewood (Gangster Disciple Territory), Nate and I got out of our cars and walked toward the front entrance. Mike had guys everywhere; some where even inside pretending to be patients! There were people standing around trying to figure out who we were. When we got to Fingers' room three bodyguards went in with us and two stood guard outside of the door. Although it was early in the morning, Mike left nothing to chance.

"What's up man? How are you feeling?" Nate asked.

"Cool, good to see you all. I hope ya'll can get me out of here. I want to get back to the house," Fingers said.

"Just wait until the doctor ok's everything," Mike added.

"He's right Fingers, just get well man. The house ain't going nowhere," Nate said assuredly.

"What exactly did the doctor say man? What's wrong with you?" Jon asked.

"Shit I don't know something about an intestinal virus or something. But I feel one-hundred percent better, no pain at all...honest," Fingers said trying to convince us.

"Yeah man but you better just wait. You'll probably be leaving next week some time," Pete said.

"Yeah. Damn you all look good! Dapper as hell. And Nate you're gonna be in GQ pretty soon!" Fingers said joyously.

"We've got some stuff at home for you, too, Fingers. Don't worry," Nate said smiling.

Truth is we hadn't gotten him anything. We just wanted to make him feel good. Fingers had no living relatives, no friends or distant family besides us. We all kind of felt sorry for him. We stood around chewing the fat with Fingers for about an hour before Mike said we had to leave. Nate gave him a hug as did all of us and we left. As we walked out of the hospital Nate sort of paused and looked up and down the street and then our entourage walked briskly to the parking lot. I noticed there where even guys on the rooftops guarding us! When it came to security, Mike was second to none. It was then that I realized just how big we all had become and we still had territories to conquer!

In the SUV Nate seemed antsy and irritated about something.

"G, when we get back to New Lenox, send some guys out to get Fingers some clothes. I don't want him getting back and finding out we all lied," Nate said. "Good job today Mike, security was tight. I liked that," Nate said admiringly.

"Yeah, no shit. I felt like the President!" Jon added.

"Do you have anything for me tonight Jon? I think I want to turn in early tonight" Nate asked.

"Not much, just that thing I talked to you and G about a few weeks ago," Jon said.

"Oh, yeah I remember. Make it brief though we got that thing coming in tomorrow and I want to get up early to prepare," Nate said.

Later when we got home Gabriella was in the family room watching television with a blanket.

"Hello honey, glad to see you. You glad to see me?" Gabriella asked talking to Nate. Nate didn't say a word. He threw his keys on the table in the foyer and started up the huge staircase.

"I'm gonna take a shower G...let me know when Jon is ready," he grumbled.

"Cool, you want a drink?" I asked as he ran up the stairs.

"I'll get one at the meeting," he said as he hugged his massive dogs sitting by the bedroom door. Gabriella abruptly got up and walked up the stairs behind Nate and into the bedroom. As she walked in, she closed the door behind them. I heard just a few words, no yelling at all, but it wasn't long before they started in heavy with the sex. A few of us heard it downstairs and we shook our heads and quietly dispersed into our various rooms in the home.

A couple of hours later Jon and I sat waiting for Nate in his office.

"What are you drinking Jon?" I asked.

"I'm not...I am smoking," Jon said smiling as he lit a huge joint he had rolled. I poured myself a cream soda and lit the fireplace in the office. "I don't know about you G, but this is the fucking life!" Jon said through his nose and smoke.

"Oh yeah?" I asked.

"Hell yeah! We're living like kings. You would be a fool to leave all of this shit," Jon snorted. I remembered our conversation on the plane to Bolivia. "Well...you still leaving or what?" Jon asked.

"No, I can't leave my brother with you clowns. He'd be in jail in a week," I said trying not to smile.

"Fuck you G," Jon said giving me the finger. Jon was really entertaining when he was high. Nate always said that's when he turned black.

"What's up guys? Let's get started," Nate said as he walked in. He had on a black silk robe with his chest exposed, a drink in his hand and one of those damn dogs!

"C'mon man with that damn dog! Do you really need her in here?" I asked disgruntled.

"Yes G. She's the only woman I completely trust. Right baby?" He asked as he rubbed the black beast under the chin and neck. "Ok Jon what's up"? Jon put out his joint and sat up and handed us both a folder with a map of Africa in it, and some countries circled.

"We going to Africa?" I asked.

"No, but I think our money should. Let's face it, we don't know how long this is gonna last. I think we should start sending some cash abroad," Jon explained.

"Yeah, but why Africa, why not the Caribbean?" Nate asked.

"Too U.S. friendly. The fucking Justice Department would have our money ten minutes after the first deposit. Fuck the Caribbean. Africa is the way to go fellas," Jon said.

"Doesn't the U.S. keep track of Africa, too?" I asked.

"Please. *Nobody* keeps track of Africa. It's really fucked up over there, with all of the tribal wars, Apartheid, famine and shit. The U.S. Government and the United Nations are trying to pretend they don't know what the fuck is going on over there. Sticking their head in the sand and shit, and when they pull their heads out, we will have millions over there already. Don't you guys watch the news? I mean it's really fucked up over there! No offense," Jon cautiously added.

"None taken, ok, which countries do you suggest?" I asked. "I like Nigeria or one of the western countries. They are industrialized, but their economy is struggling. We can get about one hundred of their dollars for every one of ours!" Jon said.

"No shit? Sounds good to me. What about you G, what do you think?" Nate asked.

"Cool, but get me some info on their political setup and who's in power, and their system of banking and get back to us," I said.

"Cool I'll get back to you by next week," Jon replied picking up his joint.

"Jon did you tell the others about this?" Nate asked.

"Fuck no, they ain't interested in this shit Nate and you know it. They want to blow all of their money. They can give a damn about tomorrow!" Jon said.

"I feel you, but tell them just the same. I like to take care of my people. Plus to think that they don't care is dismissive Jon. Let's let them make up their own minds and not do it for them....understand?" Nate instructed.

"Cool man, you got it," Jon said as he lit his joint and left the room.

"That asshole thinks all of us are fucking buffoons. See when he starts smoking that shit, what he really thinks starts coming out!" Nate said pissed off.

"Ah, don't make it racial Nate. We both know he's right, Mike, Pete, Dana and the rest of them do blow a whole lot of money," I said in Jon's defense.

"Now there you go, taking up for him again and shit. You can't assume what people will do and what they won't do," Nate said.

"Well, we'll see what they do," I said conceding the discussion. "What's the setup for tomorrow?"

"I talked to Hugo and his people. The shipment should arrive at the Baltimore Inner Harbor at about 2 p.m. eastern time. Mike, Pete, and about twenty of our mafia guys are gonna leave here in a few hours heading out. Some of the Latin Kings and the Vice Lords are going to be sending some of their people with them. We are giving them a piece...not a big piece but just out of respect. You will monitor the whole thing from here. They have been instructed if anything goes wrong. I don't give a fuck if they get a flat tire, they are to call you."

"Nate, what am I supposed to do from New Lenox?" I asked.

"Just tell them how to handle whatever mess they get into, plus you and Jon have all of the intelligence at the harbor under control. You can handle it G," Nate assured.

"Why did you pick Mike and Pete?"

"They have the best driving records and Pete is gonna test the shit from there and make sure it is legit."

The next day everything went according to plan. The guys arrived at the harbor about 1:15 p.m. I kept in touch with them by phone and there were no problems anywhere. Getting drugs from the harbor in those days was like taking candy from a baby. In those days, up to ten percent of the cargo coming into U.S. ports was never checked anyway. Jon's contact checked out and the large crate was loaded onto the truck. The guys were ready to crack the crate and check the stuff out when a couple of guys from the U.S. Marshal's office and the Maryland State Police approached them. It turns out that The President was coming to Maryland for a speech and they were checking everything and everybody. What rotten timing! Needless to say the guys started to panic.

"Look just use the phony ID's we gave you and tell them you are from Customs. Jon made sure all of the paperwork was legit," I urged. The guys from the Latin Kings disguised themselves as dock workers that spoke no English and the Vice Lords disguised themselves as Jamaicans with work visas. Without Jon's contacts and his phony ID's the plan would have fell through. The U.S. Marshals checked their credentials and let them go. I instructed them not to open the crate and check the contents until they got back home. Things were going smooth except Nate was driving me crazy; he was worried like a mother hen. I had to give him a blow by blow every five minutes. Latin King and Vice Lord chieftains kept calling on the cell and asking questions; They were all pissing me off. Dana and her crew were to meet them in Indiana and guide them in with the stuff. The Latin Kings and the Vice Lords' stuff was packaged separately, so they split off near the Calumet Expressway heading back to Chicago. When they all arrived at the house, Nate helped the guys bring in the huge crate.

"Open that shit up, Pete. Did you check it out?" Nate asked.

"Naw, didn't G tell you I couldn't. We got stopped by the Marshals and shit. I didn't have time," Pete said.

"You *didn't*? What the fuck Pete? We could've been screwed! Get this shit open now!" Nate yelled. By now, he was sweating. When we finally got the crate open we all started to smell coffee. And sure enough that's what it was....coffee.

"This shit is coffee Nate!" I said.

"Get the fuck out of the way!" Nate pushed all of us out of the way and jumped on top of the crate. He plowed through the coffee with his bare hands and dug deep down in it. "There's something else in here. Get the shovels and dig that coffee out." Pete, Mike and some of the mafia guys started digging.

"Where you want us to put the coffee at Nate?" Mike asked.

"On the fucking floor, Mike. I don't give a shit. I need you all to get to that package in the middle," Nate shouted. After about ten or fifteen minutes the guys lifted the smaller more dense package out. It was vacuum packed in blue plastic. "Get that fucking scale in here," Nate barked. When it was weighed it came to 199lbs, so the weight was right. Nate jabbed a knife into the side and some white powder came out. "Get me that beaker over here. If this shit turns blue, were in business."

Nate tapped a little into the beaker and swirled it around and slowly......surely....it turned......Blue! Everyone jumped and screamed and yelled in exuberance. Dana jumped on Mike's back and pumped her fist in the air. Everyone was overflowing with emotion; Nate plopped down in a chair with the beaker in his hand. It was as if a heavy burden had been lifted off of him. Just then the phone rang, we could barely hear it.

"Wait a minute....wait everybody the phone is ringing!" I yelled. It was Alonzo; he wanted to know if everything went ok – if the shipment came. He told us that Hugo also sent about ten pounds of Heroin for the extra money we gave him and that they were gracious and looked forward to our future business together. Gabriella came downstairs and asked what was going on.

"Nothing sweetie. Go back upstairs. We're just celebrating a little," Nate answered.

"Well I want a drink, too. What happened?" she asked. Nate told her everything and she seemed happy too. I guess in her mind that meant there would be more money she could spend.

Over the next few days Nate got with Pete and organized the making of the crack. Pete had a staff of about ten and all they did was turn cocaine into crack....all day. But making cocaine to sell at the magnitude we were wasn't like making it in the kitchen with some baking soda, we used the lab! Lollie had taught Pete how to mass produce the stuff synthetically. The "Lab" as we called it was complete with Centrifuges, Electrothermal Bunsen Burners, and several huge Tupperware containers of all sizes. Lollie gave Pete a recipe that he said was sure to hook anybody. He said one "serving" should contain about 15 grams of coke, top shelf Liqueur, Cutty Scotch, mineral water, and Rexal Formula Baking powder. Nate wouldn't allow any of us in the "Lab" while Pete and the crew made the stuff which was ok with us, because the stuff smelled awful. Nate had the guys on eight-hour shifts rotating all week, even on Sundays. Nate had them producing rocks the sizes of dimes and quarters with minimal "cut". The rocks ranged from 0.1 grams to almost one-gram sizes, with the street value ranging from ten to fifty dollars per rock.

Nate also sold powder too, but only by the gram, which was going for about one-hundred twenty dollars. Nate didn't want to get into Heroin, so he gave it to the Vice Lords as a "gift"; they loved that. We went from making twenty-five thousand dollars a night to bringing in sixty-thousand a night! We bombarded the streets of Chicago with so much cocaine it was amazing. We had to construct another cash room adjacent to the first one! There was tons of cash in that house and everything was good.

Nate sent a few guys to Chicago to get Fingers. When he got home, he looked depressed.

"Hey, welcome back man...we've got a lot to tell you," I said excited.

"Oh yeah...what's up?" Fingers replied dryly.

"You ok, man? What's the matter, still drugged from the hospital?"

"I need to talk to you....somebody," he said sorrowfully.

"Come on, let's go to the office." I said putting my arm around his shoulder. Fingers went on to telling me that the doctor said that he had Herpes and syphilis. They cured the syphilis at the hospital, but he had Herpes for life. I felt so sorry for him; he looked devastated.

"What the fuck am I gonna do now G? I can't live with this shit, my life is over," Fingers sobbed.

"No it ain't man. I'm sure there are medicines on the market to treat it....you know so you can live with it," I assured.

"Yeah right. I will never get married or have children. What woman in her right mind is gonna hook up with a man that has Herpes? I must have got that shit in Bolivia from those bitches!" he said reflecting.

"Shit if that's the case, we better get the rest of the guys tested. I better let Nate know."

"No. Don't tell Nate I got this shit! I don't want everybody treating me like I got leprosy!"

"Nobody's going to treat you like that, Fingers. You're our boy...our homey for life. Cheer up and have a drink."

"I can't, the doctor says that alcohol might induce flare ups."

Then I understood the ramifications of his new life. Fingers sobbed like a baby. He went on to lament, saying that he hated his life, that he had no family, no education, and now he had Herpes for the duration. I just sat there listening to him, trying to console him the best I could, but it wasn't working. I told Nate about it and he got pissed off.

"That fucking Hugo, hooking my boys up with those tainted-ass hoes!" Nate said angrily. "Let me call his ass and tell him how I feel about this shit!" Nate was so pissed he even turned the Sox game off!

"Nate, don't do that. You would be wrong," I said softly.

"How, how the fuck am I wrong? My fucking man is down there burning because of Hugo's nasty-ass hookers! Oh, I'm supposed to just let that shit go G? Don't worry I ain't gonna screw up the business deal we got with him, I just want to tell him what is up and how I don't appreciate it, that's all!" he said aggressively.

"Ok, but before you make the call, hear me out," I said as I sat on the sofa. I scratched my head trying to find the words to make Nate hear me. "Nate as much as I don't like this either, Fingers brought this on himself. Nate, we sleep with people at our own risk...if we don't take precautions it's on us, not the people we sleep with. And in this case certainly not Hugo! Fingers took a chance. They all did and unfortunately Fingers crapped out. If not for the grace of God, Fingers could be any one of us, Nate. If you pick up that phone and call Hugo with this shit you're gonna sound like an emotional lame, and probably alter his outlook on you. Do you want to risk that? There's millions of dollars at stake. Pick your battles. This one you can't win.

Nate threw the bottle of beer he had into the fireplace with anger. He knew I was right. "What are you? A fucking psychiatrist, now? Fuck! I just don't like this shit G, I don't like it!" I quietly got up from the couch and walked toward the door to leave.

"Don't make that call, Nate," I said as I left the room.

Fingers sank deeper into depression. Upon learning of his illness, we all tried to make life easier for him…keep his spirits up. None of it worked. Dana, Mike, and Pete took him to the Taste of Chicago to try and lift him up, then shopping afterward. When they got home Fingers seemed a little happier – relieved almost.

"Hey now that's what I'm talking about – you're smiling. How was everything?" I asked.

"Cool G, we had a good time, man. That Dana is crazy, she almost got into a fight at the Taste can you believe that?" he asked.

"Yeah, I know Dana. You didn't eat too much, did you?" I asked.

"Hell yeah, I am stuffed. I think I'm gonna lie down for a few hours…until dinner tonight. Wake me up around seven-thirty."

"Cool."

After he went upstairs Mike told me how he had a great time and seemed like the old Fingers; I was relieved to hear it. Gabriella came downstairs and told us that she told the cooks to make stir fry tonight – Fingers' favorite meal. I thought that was nice of her. Nate and I had a couple of meetings to attend. Then later Jon and Nate left for a meeting with some "associates" in Manooka. When they returned we all got together to eat. Fingers had been sleep most of the day. Gabriella set the huge dinette table for all of us to eat together with Fingers. Dana even put on a skirt for the occasion! Nate got washed up and told Dana to go and wake Fingers; that it was about time to eat. The food looked great and smelled even better. Gabriella went out and purchased expensive Chinaware and silver utensils; the table was fabulous. After about ten minutes or so Nate yelled upstairs.

"Hey Dana could you two hurry up? We're hungry as hell down here!" he said. Dana rushed  down the staircase with a puzzled look on her face.

"Did you wake him up?" I asked.

"I tried…I can't. He won't wake up. I think ya'll need to go upstairs."

"The fuck you mean you can't wake him up?" Nate said. We all hopped up the stairs to Fingers' room and found him sprawled across the bed. "Fingers wake up man!" Nate yelled. I walked toward him and felt his head. It was cool to the touch. I saw an empty pill bottle on the floor next to the bed and about three lines of unsnorted coke on a mirror on the nightstand. Nate and Mike flipped him over and his nose had dried blood on it. Fingers had committed suicide. "He's gone," Nate said as he cradled Fingers' head on his lap.

"Damn," Dana said. Gabriella started to cry and walked out of the room. Nate kissed the top of his head and told me to call the appropriate people.

"Damn Fingers, why man?" Mike asked between sobs.

"He couldn't take it...he just couldn't take it," Pete said. Dana saw a note he had written on the dresser and read it.

*"What's up guys? I just wanted you all to know I love you all. You were the family I never had. The last few years have been the best, but I can't live with this disease. I know you all can't understand, and I hope you never will be forced to. I've had a nice life and don't have any regrets. Thanks G for being there for me on those difficult nights...man, I appreciate it. Ya'll be good. I love you. Your homey for life....Cordell."*

We were heartbroken. Nate and I made arrangements to have him buried at Oak Woods Cemetery in Chicago, where mamma Williams and my mother were. It was tough to lose another one of our friends. Donnell had been gone for years, but Fingers' death brought it all back. Nate and I hung around after the burial with some of our bodyguards and reflected. We decided to visit mamma Williams and my mother before we left.

"I really miss them, G. It's been tough these past few years," Nate said wiping a tear away.

"Yeah, how have you been Nate? You handling everything ok?" I asked concerned.

"Yeah, just Gabriella driving me crazy". He said smiling.

"Yeah, you two were made for each other...two knuckleheads." We both stood over my mother's grave for a minute in silence.

"You know she's pregnant G?" Nate said out of nowhere.

"Really, congratulations, man, that's great!" I said as I threw my arm around him and slapped him on the chest.

"Thanks man, but what kind of father am I gonna be?" Nate said in deep thought. Then Detective Jackson and a few cops walked toward us.

"What the fuck does she want?" Nate asked disgusted.

"Just to harass us probably."

"Hello boys, I know this is not the best time in the world, but this has to be done. Nathan Williams, you are under arrest for the murder of Lawrence Caldwell. You have the right to remain silent, anything you say can be held......," she recited proudly.

"What is this shit? You can't arrest him now and this is a fucking funeral!" I said as I motioned for the bodyguards to stand down.

"It's cool G, you know what to do. It'll be ok," Nate said surprisingly subdued. Mike was also arrested at the bottom of the hill as an accessory to the crime.

"I told you I'd get you guys Derek...I warned you before," she said with a smirk.

"You just made the biggest mistake of your fucking career detective," I said while gritting my teeth.

## CHAPTER 3

## ...AND JUSTICE FOR ALL

After Detective Jackson pulled that, I had to scramble to take care of things. Jon got on the phone immediately to some of our "associates"; and I had Dana and Pete take care of any problems with the business and around the house. Jon came back and told me that they would arraign Nate early the next morning. The state wanted Nate held without bail, because they felt he might be involved in the drug rackets.

"They are gonna arraign him in the morning. I made some arrangements and he will be placed into protective custody until the arraignment; after that, he goes into general population," Jon explained.

"What about Mike? What are they gonna do with him?" I asked.

"Same deal. They are gonna get the same deal, except Mike won't be held anywhere near Nate. We will just have to hope for the best," Jon said.

"Hope my ass...I have never trusted those motherfuckers at the County Jail. They're full of shit!" Dana said.

I just looked out of the window thinking. Thinking of what to do if Nate was denied bail, and what to do if bail was set. Then Gabriella came into the office.

"Will they set him free for the trial? How do they do things here?" she asked me concerned. After I explained the judicial process, she had a look of confusion on her face. I guess with being pregnant and in a strange country, she just felt lost. "Help me get my Nathan back please, G. Do whatever you guys have to do. I don't want to lose him." She started sobbing.

"We all are going to work very hard Gabby. We have lawyers and we will use all of our power to get him back. But let us handle it you just try to relax. You're in your first trimester and you don't need to be upset," I explained.

"I am going upstairs to call my mother. Keep me in touch, ok?" she said.

"Sure, but let Pete get you a secured line, ok?" I said. She complied and walked up the stairs. She was very cooperative during the whole process; I guess pregnancy changes women. Jon had been gone for a while gathering the intelligence info I told him I needed and I gathered what I could from home on the phone. The thing I worried about the most was that Nate would be denied bail. I got our lawyers to work the judge and try to get him anything. I knew in my mind that if Nate went to general population, the gangster disciples would kill him. I couldn't let that happen. I laid up half the night figuring and planning our next move. I was really afraid.

The next morning we were told that we should be at the Dirkson Federal Building courthouse by 9:30 a.m. with our lawyers. I made sure the lawyers were there in the parking lot by 7 o'clock. I wasn't taking any chances that the system may arraign Nate at eight and no one be there to argue bail for him. Me, Jon, Dana, and Pete arrived at eight; Gabriella was urged to stay home in case things got intense – she could be very emotional at times. We all walked into the courtroom and sat on the benches behind our defense attorneys and held hands. I desperately needed for Nate to get bail; we would figure out how to fight the case later. Nate walked in accompanied by two sheriffs with his hands cuffed behind his back. Then

Detective Jackson walked in with her partner, both gleaming. Dana whispered to me that the detective was a fucking bitch. I told her that we needed to be cool and maintain our composure in the courtroom. After all of the formalities the state's attorney presented his case for Nate to be held without bail. He went described the nature of the crime and rumors of Nate's involvement in drug rackets.

Our attorney objected, stating that Nate's criminal record was pristine and that rumors were no grounds for remanding Nate. After much negotiating between the prosecution and our lawyers with a couple of interruptions from the judge, he made his decision.

"The defendant's has no record from what I can see, not even a moving violation. However the nature of this crime as well as the case presented by the prosecution is serious. Therefore I will set bail at two-hundred thousand dollars, with a tentative trial date for........November 2$^{nd}$ of this year."

As Nate walked out of the room, he gave us a quick look and a wink of the eye. Detective Jackson was pissed; she abruptly got up and stormed out of the courtroom. I was so relieved, but I noticed that Mike was never brought out for his arraignment. When we got outside we were told by the lawyers that the charges against Mike were dropped, due to lack of evidence. That was strange; if there was a lack of evidence, why did they arrest him in the first place? I had Jon stay and post the twenty-thousand, and we all left. When we got home Nate took his clothes off, got a drink and came into the office where we were all supposed to meet.

"Where's Jon? He isn't back yet?" he asked me.

"Nah, he's supposed to be returning with the lawyers. They are meeting with the prosecution to try and find out just what they have," I explained. "How did they treat you in there?"

"*Shit*, like a criminal.  I can't believe that bitch arrested me at the cemetery.  She must have been following us the whole time."

"They dropped the charges against Mike, supposed to be lack of evidence, what do you think about that?"

"They didn't want him really.  Why else would they drop his charges?  I wonder what they have."

"Who knows?  The lawyers will let us know everything tonight.  Just try to relax...is Gabby ok?" I asked concerned.

"Yeah, she talked to her mother tonight.  Her mom's so afraid she's gonna get killed up here.  She told her mom she was pregnant and that just made everything worse.  She was very happy to see me, but now that I have this case hanging over me, who knows what tomorrow will bring?  Shit I need a joint, you got anything?"

"Nah, Dana will be down in a minute...she's always got some stuff."  Dana gave Nate a joint and he picked up his cell phone, a 9mm, and took his dogs out for a walk. He insisted he wanted to be alone, but I sent some mafia guys to go with him anyway.  I went into his office and poured myself a Cognac and pulled out a pad and a pen and started trying to figure out what moves to make.  It was futile though, I couldn't begin to map out a strategy until I knew what the state had on Nate.  Dana came into the office and sat down on the couch with a bottle of beer and a joint of her own.  It was around ten-thirty when the doorbell rang.  The house staff answered it and let the guys in.  Jon, Mike, and a couple of our lawyers came in and poured themselves drinks in the office.  Everyone looked glum and defeated.  "Ok, what's up...what do they have?

Better yet, don't answer that until Nate gets back. He'll want to hear it, too," I said.

"You know those miserable motherfuckers didn't have a thing on me. They just wanted to see if I would give them anything on Nate. Once they saw I wasn't gonna talk, they let me go," Mike said smiling.

"*Really?* They really dropped all of the charges on you?" Dana asked.

"Yeah, but I'll tell you one thing, that Jackson broad has a real hard-on for Nate. She wants him in jail bad. She interrogated me by herself for two hours before letting her partner at me. I just don't understand it," Mike said.

"I wish these assholes would be this hard up to find Titus. I mean he was accused of killing a convenience store full of white folks less than three months ago, and the heat on that is already beginning to die down," Pete said walking into the room.

I gave him an eye shot to be quiet since the lawyers were still in the room. I didn't want anyone saying anything incriminating around them. Who knows who they are working for? Nate came into the house and sent the dogs upstairs. After looking in on Gabby, he came into the office.

"Ok, let's have it. What do they have?" he said after letting out a deep sigh.

"An eyewitness – they have a guy who said he was stopped at a light and saw the whole thing. He fingered you from a group of pictures Jackson gave him. He says you're the killer. Now Nate it's our job to give you counsel. We met with the prosecution and we made a tentative deal for second degree…and we think you should take it," the lawyer advised.

"Second degree? Ok, so what are we looking at?" I asked.

"Twenty years…you'll do ten, but that's the best offer we could get for you. I mean they have an eyewitness. We're good at creating reasonable doubt, but it's hard to create that doubt when the jury is looking at a man who is saying he saw you. What I'm saying is…it's hard when the other guys have an eyewitness."

"Fuck, this is bullshit!" Nate yelled.

"Wait a minute Nate. Look, without the witness, what do they have?" I asked the lawyer.

"Not much. They have some testimonies from some questionable sources, but we could cut through that like a hot knife through butter. They were hoping to get more from Michael, but he really didn't give them anything more so they let him go," the lawyer said.

"Ok, do you have anything else for us? Anything that you could help us with?" I asked the lawyers.

"Not really. The state gave us until Monday to make a decision on the offer. You guys got three days to get back to us with a decision. Derrick, it's the best offer we could get."

"Ok, we thank you for all you have done. We really do." I said standing up and showing them to the door. They stood up, sat their drinks down, shook our hands, and left. "Fucking lawyers! They're as crooked as a barrel of snakes," I said when they were gone.

"You think they're in on it G?" Nate asked.

"Shit I don't know…maybe, but I just don't like the way these assholes make deals with people's lives and talk about you doing ten years in jail like it's no big deal," I replied.

"Yeah, but they did the best they could under the circumstances G," Pete said.

"Fuck them! Whether Nate does ten years or dies, they still get paid," I shot back.

"Ok look, it's late. Let's all get some sleep and we will figure this out in the morning. Jon get as much info as you can on Detective Jackson and this case. I will get my intelligence people on the street to give me all they can on this "eyewitness" they have and we will come up with a strategy. Let's meet tomorrow night," I said.

Everyone dispersed and went to bed. Nate patted me on the back and told me everything would be alright as he left the room. But with the look on his face, I don't think even he believed it. We were in trouble – all of us if Nate went to jail. They would come after all of us and we all knew it. This was a scary time.

I took a shower and then lay in the bed wondering how to handle this situation. I knew this time I was going to have to get *my* hands dirty, but I couldn't let my brother go to jail. Nate wouldn't last a week in jail and we all knew it. He had made so many enemies over the last few years and most of those guys were in jail waiting for him. Not to mention the Gangster Disciples, those fucking guys were probably salivating.

The next morning I had some guys go get me the newspapers. I knew Jackson would have it in the news, I just hoped it wouldn't be front page stuff. Sure enough it was in the news, but not a cover story. Fortunately for us there was news in town of much more importance. Cook County political powerhouse George Dunne was accused of making two women sleep with him to keep their jobs at the Forest Preserves...bad news for them, good news for us.

"Now you see this shit G? This motherfucker trying to make these women sleep with his decrepit ass to keep their jobs...politicians ain't shit!" Dana exclaimed. I smiled as I sipped my coffee; my mind was somewhere else. Gabby came downstairs with Nate for breakfast and we all ate and talked lightly. Nate announced that he and Gabriella were getting married; we all clapped and were genuinely happy for them. Dana made a sarcastic remark and Gabriella started in on her. Their many arguments were irritating usually, but it gave all of us a sense of normalcy that we needed. By the end of the day intelligence information started coming in.

One of my top sources, Cisco, always had the best and most reliable information.

"What you know good, nigga? It's been a while," Cisco said giving me a hug.

"Too long. Come on in have a drink," I said inviting him and his people in.

"Ok, what you got for me?" I asked. He told me everything he knew: about Detective Jackson; how bad she wanted us all; and how she had a hunch on our drug affiliations, but was frustrated because she couldn't prove it.

"Why does she want you all so bad man?" he asked reaching for some cocktail shrimp.

"Shit...I don't know man...trying to make a name for herself I guess. What's the word on the street, Cisco?"

"Everybody's in wait and see mode. If Nate goes to jail, they will eat your flesh. If he beats the case and doesn't go to jail; he's the king of Chicago" he said plainly.

"Yeah, I understand how it goes. What else you got?"

"Not much.....oh yeah, your boy Jon got offered a high profile job at the bank, an underwriter I think."

"Did he take it?"

"Don't know, but I know he go offered."

"Cool, I'll check it out. Thanks for everything man. If you get anything else let me know."

Cisco let me also know that Detective Jackson had a son that likes to get high. I checked all of our dealers and found that he was a regular buyer of refer from a guy of ours on the south side. But the best intelligence came later that night from one of our inside police operatives…information that *had* to be shared with the rest of the family later that night.

"Ok, everybody listen up. I got information on the eyewitness and other shit," I said. Pete had one of the guys go out for Chinese takeout and we were all sitting around Nate's office eating and planning. "Jon, I heard you got offered a job at the bank…you not bailing out on us are you?" I asked sarcastically. Everyone was so surprised they stopped eating.

"No….hell no, G. I turned them cats down man. Shit, I don't want to work in no bank, you know that," Jon said nervously.

"Shit I *don't* know. Maybe you thought about getting out while the getting is good. It's not like you told us about the offer," I replied.

"G, I actually forgot all about it. With all this shit going on…..I just forgot," Jon said. Everyone was starting to look at Jon strangely, wondering if they could trust him. "Nate I would never turn on you man, I have already risked my life for the family…you know that. It was just a bullshit job offer man, that's all. You all can trust me!" Jon said emphatically.

"Ah, it's no big deal G. Jon is loyal, he always was. Plus Jon knows the rules. Any defectors will die, no matter who, right Jon?" Nate asked.

"Yeah, right," Jon said cautiously.

"Ah, let's do business. We'll worry about all of that later," Nate said.

"Ok, my man Cisco and my other contacts said this "eyewitness" that says they saw Nate is a guy named Dr. Paul McFadden. He says he saw Nate cut Larry C's throat while he was stopped at a traffic light," I said. Then one of our operatives from the mafia spoke up on some background on the guy.

"He's on staff at two hospitals. We found out his criminal record is clean and his reputation in the medical community is impeccable," the operative stated.

"Any family, wife, children?" Nate asked.

"Wife died of leukemia two years ago. He has a daughter that is about five months pregnant and lives with him," the operative stated.

"What about a husband? Is she married?" Mike asked.

"They're separated. He stays away on business and he owns a fast food chain down south," the operative said. Speculation started swirling around the room as to how we were going to handle it. Everyone was talking at once to each other while they ate. Mike wanted Nate to leave town; Dana thought we should kill the doctor; Pete thought we should shut the operation down; Jon talked about plea bargaining; and Nate just listened to all of the theories. I was sitting there in my own thoughts; I knew what they were suggesting would never work. After much bickering and disagreeing, people started to lean toward Dana's idea of killing the doctor.

"We can't do that. That's exactly what the prosecution and most of the cops in this city expect us to do. We would be playing right into their hands. Is this doctor a black man?" I asked the operative.

"Yeah, middle-aged I would say," he answered. Everyone looked at me waiting for my response, even Nate seemed to be anticipating it. Then something came over me, something dark and sinister.

"Ok, this is what we will do. We have to get him to change his story. Dana, I want you to get to his daughter, take her to a location…somewhere discreet, maybe one of our safe houses, but make sure she is blindfolded so she won't know where she is. Don't do any harm to her until you get the word from us. I want you to strip her naked and tie her down to a bed or something. Mike, you video tape the whole thing. We need Dana in a ski mask or disguised in some way and we will let the doctor know that if he doesn't change his story we will kill his daughter and his unborn grandchild. But if he changes it, they will be allowed to live and we will pay him one million dollars into an offshore account for this choice."

"That's risky G. You think we can pull it off? I mean I'm sure Detective Jackson has him guarded at all times expecting something like that," Nate said.

"What choice do we have? The only way we can keep you from going to jail is if he changes his story," I said.

"It might work. The word is Detective Jackson had to talk to him for a week to get him to testify. He really didn't want to get involved," the operative added. Nate let out a deep sigh, shrugged his shoulders, and asked everyone what they thought. Everyone agreed it was our best and only chance. It was a gamble, but a gamble we had to take.

"Ok, everybody let's move," I said.

**Chicago Police Headquarters (The next morning):**

"Ok, Dr. McFadden, nobody knows you are testifying on our behalf and nobody has to know. Keep a low profile and I will keep security around you as much as possible. You are our key witness; everything will be ok…you'll see," Jackson assured.

"I really don't want to do this, I really don't," the doctor said nervously.

"You are going to help us get a murderer off the street. You are doing the community a service. If you don't speak out, there is a good chance this scum will go free, and I know you don't want that," Jackson said.

"No…I don't but….," the doctor said.

"Dr. McFadden, everything will be alright, trust me," Jackson said calmly.

"Jackson…Inspector needs to see you," A young detective said with a cigarette in his mouth.

"Tell him in a minute, I am preparing a witness," Jackson said without looking up.

"No…now!" The detective said vehemently.

Jackson slapped her hands on her desk, rose up angrily, and stormed out of the room. She wondered what Inspector Trent wanted that was so important.

"Yes sir, you needed to see me?" she asked.

"Absolutely, come in and close the door," Trent said. "I want to personally congratulate you on this case. I hear your witness is working out fine."

"Yeah, I think I have this guy where I want him now – as soon as I hang his ass on this murder, I'm going after his alleged drug affiliations," Jackson said proudly.

"Good, but let me give you a word of advice detective: step slowly. A lot can happen between an arrest and a conviction," Trent warned.

"What do you mean boss?" Jackson asked puzzled.

"Well I mean take it slowly. I don't want you to end up out there in the wind again that's all. I don't think you or the department can afford that," Trent said.

"In the wind? I have a legitimate witness, an eyewitness I might add, and a respectable one. He's a doctor and his reputation in the medical community here in Chicago is without a blemish. That piece-of-shit-murdering Nathan Williams is going down this time; him and his cohort brother, Derrick, and that whole operation of theirs!" Jackson said defensively and agitated. Detective Trent looked at Jackson long and hard.

"Close the door detective, I want to tell you something," Trent said after a pregnant pause. Jackson closed the door to the stuffy office with reluctance. "You be very careful in your quest for justice with these two kids. They are slippery, cunning and extremely crafty. Nathan Williams is tough and he's smart…and that brother of his is even smarter. We've been watching them for quite some time. They are not going to go down without a fight, so you be very careful," Trent warned.

"I appreciate that Inspector, but they are at a disadvantage now. This witness saw the whole thing in the park, and he's willing to testify to that," Jackson said trying to compose herself.

"I still say detective. A lot can happen between arrest and conviction….be careful," Trent said.

"Excuse me for saying this Inspector, but you sound like you are on their side! I mean like you are afraid of them or something."

"What the hell is that supposed to mean?"

"I don't know boss…you seem to be a little touchy when it comes to these guys, and you always have been. I would expect you to be giving me all of the info and encouragement I need in this case and all I get from you is warnings. I have applied for surveillance authority, extra men, warrants and I have been met with a bunch of bureaucracy and red tape from your office."

"That's bullshit and you know it. I have given you access to whatever you have asked for!" Trent said clearly offended.

"No sir, I think you are protecting these guys....everyone knows about you and Gloria Williams, the boys' mother, and....." Jackson said before Trent sharply cut her off.

"What the fuck did you just say to me? Let me tell you something hot-shot-ass detective. This has nothing to do with Gloria Williams, or some fantasy that I am protecting these boys. This has to do with your wild escapades and the fact that you have a propensity for making arrests and not being able to turn them into convictions! Fifty-two arrests in the last two years, twelve convictions, only twelve! Get this through your head, Jackson. You will not continue to embarrass this department with your shoddy work! You go for those boys, but if you fuck it up, I will have your ass! Do you understand me?" Trent said angrily.

"Look Inspector, I....." Jackson said before she was interrupted.

"Goodbye detective!" Trent shouted. As detective Jackson walked out of the office, she noticed many were standing around the area pretending not to be listening. Some were looking and whispering. She felt betrayed by her superior officer. She was also convinced that he may be involved in helping them for some strange reason, but she didn't care. With an eyewitness, his help or anyone else's was of no consequence. She just had to make sure Dr. McFadden was safe and secure until trial date.

**New Lenox**

"Ok, when do we get started? I mean we have a few months before trial, should we wait?" Mike asked as he sipped from a bottle of beer.

"Absolutely...no reason to start anything too soon. I have some guys watching Jackson and the doctor; and they will let us know what's going on and when we can make our move," I replied. Then one of the mafia members gently knocked on the door and asked to speak to me. He told me that we had an informant within the ranks. He told me that Pookie, Dana's trusted confidant, had a couple of secret meetings with one of Jackson's men, feeding him information. Luckily for us our plans had not been relayed to anyone outside of the inner circle. When I told Nathan about it, he was livid, and Dana wanted to kill Pookie that night.

"This shit is getting stickier by the minute. Motherfuckers are turning coat already," Nate said.

"I can't believe Pookie. He's been so loyal," Dana said.

"I can believe it. *Shit!* If he would turn on the Disciples what would keep him from turning on us?" Pete said.

We were losing allies from all ranks – from the Latin Kings, Vice Lords and some of the friendly drug distributors were running from us. It wasn't personal. That's what happens when you get heat on you. In our business it pays to stay in the shadows. I believe the cats cared; they just didn't want any heat on them. One thing they could take comfort in, they knew none of us would rat them out; they knew Nate was a true gangster and true gangsters don't rat out their friends in the business. But the Gangster Disciples weren't wasting a golden opportunity like this. We got word from our people that some of our dealers on the street were being whacked out and robbed by GD's. We even lost some of our mafia guys in the struggle. Nate and I were told that after one of their recent parties, some area GD's sprayed some of our guys on the street in front of their homes killing about six of Dana's guys and nine or ten of Mike's. We wanted to fight back, but we couldn't. Retaliation would only put more spotlight and heat on us than we could afford.

The guys I had watching the doctor were simply told to document his habits – what he did and when he did them – and report back to us. The doctor lived a boring life according to reports. He only went to work and than back home. Occasionally he would go fishing, but nothing more. The reports that came back for Detective Jackson were much better. She was seeing some guy, and we found out that her son liked to get high….on marijuana. We decided to use that to our advantage.

"Ok, let's get someone to plant some drugs on this kid of hers. How old is he?" Nate asked.

"Nineteen…he's kind of hanging around the city; going to parties; fucking around with broads on the south side; shit like that. He keeps a low profile, not running around letting everyone know Jackson is his mother," Mike said.

"Doesn't matter, shit we know now. Get somebody on that motherfucker, G. I want to know his habits and hangouts, too," Nate said.

"When do we get started G?" Mike asked.

"Well there is a pre-trial hearing next month. We'll get the feel for how relaxed the prosecution is and then we'll get started," I said.

At the pretrial hearing we found out that Jackson had pulled out all of the stops.

"We will begin our hearing on the case number 689761463, the state of Illinois vs. Nathan Williams on the charge of murder in the first degree. Counselor you may begin," The judge said.

Detective Jackson sat a couple of rows behind the prosecution gleaming with pride. There were members in the courtroom from Larry C's family, from the community, and some of the press. The courtroom was dank and dimly lit with a large echo emanating from the microphones as people spoke. Nate wore a crisp, navy blue Armani suit with lilac accessories, and crocodile black shoes. We all wore suits and Dana wore a cream-colored Vera Wang two-piece suit with matching pumps. We all looked very classy. The prosecution was throwing everything, but the kitchen sink at Nate. They even implied that he was involved in the drug rackets.

"Your honor the man is sitting in the courtroom with a six-thousand dollar suit on and he is unemployed!" The prosecutor said. Things were going Jackson's way in the hearings, plus we were feeding Pookie false information to give to her until Nate decided it was time to cancel Pookie's contract.

"It's time to get rid of this motherfucker, before he gives her something we won't be able to recover from," Nate said.

"Yeah, but let's do it carefully. A body cannot be found," I said. Dana, Mike, and Jon went out for their usual trip to get chicken at Harold's Chicken Shack and took Pookie along.

"Get me a quarter dark meat with extra mild sauce, Mike," Pookie said as he sat in the front seat of the truck. When Mike got out of the truck, Dana struck Pookie over the head and knocked him out from behind. Dana stuffed a rag dampened with kerosene into his mouth and placed a plastic bag over his head and tied it at the neck; then she beat him in the head and face unmercifully with a hammer.

"Rat motherfucker!" She said after killing him. Pookie's body was taken to the south side to a funeral director. Nate had made a deal with him to cremate bodies we took to him for fifteen grand a pop; no one ever saw Pookie again. When they returned, I immediately asked about Pookie.

"Did you guys take care of that?" I asked.

"Oh yeah, that's done and over with," Mike said casually.

"Did you do it the way we talked about?" Nate asked.

"Don't worry it's all taken care of, now can we eat?" Dana said. As they all pulled out their chicken bags and sat at the dining room table, Gabriella came waddling down the stairs now visibly pregnant. She had been eating everything that hadn't been nailed down.

"Smells good…what is that?" she asked.

"Harold's," Dana said in between bites.

"Harold? Who is Harold?" Gabriella asked.

"Harold's Chicken! You never heard of Harold's? Nate you need to take her out more!" Dana said laughing. Nate smiled as he bit into an apple. Gabriella kept looking at them eat apparently interested, but hesitant to ask for a bite. "Do you want some?" Dana finally asked.

"Well….just a little. The baby is hungry," Gabby said.

"That ain't the baby, that's your ass!" Dana said. As Gabriella took the chicken leg from Dana she looked at it strangely and took a bite.

"Ugghh, it's greasy!" she said as she spit it out. Dana looked at Mike strangely as if she couldn't believe what she heard.

"It's supposed to be greasy bitch, it's Harold's! Black folks don't like no dry ass chicken!" Dana said with food in her mouth.

"Fuck you bitch! Who the hell you talking to?" Gabriella said angrily, as she began to curse Dana in Spanish.

"Hey, Hey, Hey! That's enough!" Nate said.

"You know there's no more gin? Who drank all of the gin?" Jon asked.

"I don't drink gin, but just go get a bottle," Pete said.

"No...let's you and I go Nate, I've got some stuff to talk to you about anyway," I interjected.

"You sure G, it's a little late," Nate asked.

"It's cool, we'll take some of the mafia guys with us," I assured him.

"If you all are going, bring back some popcorn, diet pop, lettuce, and...," Gabriella said before Nate interrupted her.

"We ain't going grocery shopping. Make a list out for tomorrow," Nate said closing the door behind him. In the car I wanted to keep things casual and just talk shop before hitting Nate with what I really wanted to ask him. "Look at this shit G, I told these motherfuckers not to park these trucks on empty! Now we gotta go get gas, dammit!" Nate said angrily.

"What else is new? I talked to Jon and he is starting some businesses in the community that will be owned by you and I, to try and wash some of this money. Nothing big, just beauty shops, barber shops, car washes, dance clubs, stuff like that," I said.

"Good idea. Did you hear that DA talking about how much money my suit cost and shit, like he saw the price tag," Nate said with a chuckle. As we pulled up to the gas station I checked and I forgot to bring my money.

"Nate, could you get the gas? I forgot my wallet," I said. Nate gave me a sarcastic look and got out of the truck. I looked around, as we walked to the entrance, trying to keep notice of our surroundings. The mafia guys were with us, but it was a habit I formed. While walking a familiar voice called out to us.

"Derrick, Nathan....how are you guys doing?" the older gentleman said. It was Minister Fischer, from the hospital when mamma Williams died a few years earlier.

"Hi Reverend Fischer, how have you been? It's good to see you!" I said with surprise.

"What's up, Rev.?" Nate greeted dryly. As the Minister Fischer walked toward us, the mafia guys got between us and prepared to physically back the minister away from getting too close.

"It's ok. He's ok," I said quietly.

"My...you boys have certainly grown up to be fine young men. I can see God has blessed you well," he said with a smile.

"Yeah whatever," Nate said disrespectfully.

"Don't mind him; he's a little under the weather Reverend," I said covering for Nate's rudeness and shooting him a hard look.

"What about you? How have you been?" I asked.

"Well, my health isn't the best, but God is able, right?" he asked with a smile.

"He sure is!" I said. I did notice that Reverend Fischer looked older and a little tired. Nate had walked away, paid for the gas and walked out to pump, leaving me there talking.

"Derrick, this is my son Jeremiah. He has recently accepted his call to the ministry. Jeremiah this is Derrick, an old friend," Fischer said with pride. I told him I was pleased to meet him, but I couldn't help notice how he looked around to find where Nate had gone. "Do you boys live or work out here now?" Rev asked.

I had to think quickly. I didn't want to lie to a man of God, but I couldn't exactly tell him the truth either.

"A little of both Reverend; we are working hard," I said.

"Good, hey why don't you two visit church with us one Sunday? I would love to have you out," he asked.

"Well...we work a lot on Sundays, and we are very busy Reverend," I said sheepishly.

"You should never be too busy for the Lord, son. Do you still have my card?" he asked.

"Yeah, it's in my wallet, but I left it at home," I said embarrassed.

"Well here's another. Now you hold on to this one ok?" he said in a fatherly tone.

"Ok, it was good to see you again and nice meeting you Jeremiah," I said. Jeremiah nodded and extended his hand for a shake. We exchanged pleasantries and parted ways. I always had respect for Reverend Fischer. He had a calm fatherly demeanor that emanated from him. When I got outside, I saw Reverend Fischer wave his hand at Nate as they drove off into the night. Nate held his hand up and gave a bullshit wave, but as they drove out of sight, Nate changed his wave into a middle finger gesture. As I came out of the store, I let him have it.

"You ignorant asshole! How could you treat him like that? This guy has never been nothing but good to us, and you go and treat the guy like that? What's wrong with you?" I said angrily.

"Him...that guy prayed for my mother to die, so she could be in so-called Heaven, and I'm supposed to like him? He helped take my mom from me! He's full of shit," Nate said with disgust.

"Nate you shouldn't say that about a man of God. He's a squared guy Nate. We might need him one day; you never know. How many truly squared guys do you know Nate? Probably none. That guy could help us one day," I said trying to talk sense into him.

"He gives me the fucking creeps, and I ain't feeling him! And what about your phony ass? 'Yes Reverend praise the Lord!' he said mocking me.

"I respect the man Nate. He's been cool every time I see him. And don't you believe in God?" I asked.

"Yeah I guess so, but I don't believe in no damn church and men and shit. Out here robbing all of these people, lying and shit. That's why I don't go to church," he said.

"That's bullshit Nate and you know it, and how do you know what's going on in church where you haven't been in years?" I asked him.

"Everybody knows! It ain't no secret!" he said emphatically.

"Aw you don't know shit. That's a bullshit reason you and all of these other people use not to go to church. If everything was perfect in church your ass still wouldn't go!" I said. Surprisingly Nate didn't say a word. He had a scowl on his face and just kept driving. I couldn't believe it; I finally won an argument with this guy!

When we got back to the house, Nate walked ahead of me and threw his keys on the table and went upstairs. He didn't even speak to anyone.

"Damn who pissed in his Cheerios?" Dana asked.

"Fuck him. Look we have to get up early tomorrow; I want to brief everyone on our next move," I said as I walked upstairs to my room. Later that night I lay in bed looking out of the window at the sky. I thought about how surprised I was that Nate still held mamma Williams' death against Rev. Fischer. I needed a woman tonight I thought. So I called one of my "trusties" and drank a cognac waiting for her to show up. Reverend Fischer popped into my head again. I kept wondering why he always seemed to just drop into our lives; I knew there was a reason. But the way we were living, I couldn't figure out why or how a minister could ever fit into it. Gabriella knocked on the door.

"G, you have a visitor downstairs in the foyer," she said with her Bolivian accent.

"Thanks Gabby," I said as I got up to put my robe on.

"Why don't you get a real woman, and settle your ass down and stop sleeping with whores," she said disgustingly.

"Stay out of my business Gabby," I said as I walked past her. *Humph...I wish I could tell her about some of her man's "exploits,"* I thought.

The next morning began as it usually does, everyone coming downstairs to eat breakfast together and lightly discussing a little shop talk.

"Alright G when are we gonna start this Dr. McFadden shit? And if he fucks up are we really gonna kill his daughter?" Mike asked.

"Well...," I said before Gabby interrupted me.

"Don't discuss that shit at the breakfast table please,".she said with disgust. Nate looked up and gave us a hand signal to hold it down until later. Dana slept late, this morning because she and Mike had stayed up watching television. She was never much of a morning person anyway. Gabriella was particularly irritable this morning; Dana being around only would have led to an argument.

Nate unfolded his newspaper and turned to the sports section to see how his White Sox were doing.

"Look at this shit, the Sox are on a five game winning streak and still the fucking stands are half empty!" he said.

"Shit the Cubs sell out every day, whether they lose or win. I've always liked them better anyway," Mike said before catching himself.

"You what? I didn't know you liked the fucking Cubs, when did that shit start?" Nate asked.

"Well.....I always did Nate. I never said anything because I know you are a Sox fan," Mike said sheepishly. Nate picked up his plate and utensils and went to eat upstairs.

"Where are you going?" Gabriella asked.

"In my room...I don't eat with no fucking Cub fans," Nate said as he stomped up the stairs.

"Don't be ridiculous; come back here and eat," Gabby pleaded.

"One big happy family," Pete said sarcastically.

"What is this shit? Don't the Cubs and the Sox play for Chicago?" Gabby asked.

"Well...yeah, but Sox and Cubs fans don't get along well," I said.

"That is the most ridiculous shit I have ever heard," she said laughing. Then Dana came walking downstairs into the kitchen, and started making her plate. She wiped her eyes, and threw a piece of bacon into her mouth. As she walked past Gabriella, she closed her robe and plopped down into the chair.

"Morning ya'll," she said still groggy.

"Don't you ever brush your teeth in the morning before you put food into it?" Gabby asked. Dana didn't even look her way and just gave her the finger.

"What time do we meet today G?" she asked with a deep sleep voice.

"One o'clock. You gonna be on time or what?" I asked smiling.

"Yeah, I'll make it. I stayed up with this fool last night watching a movie," she said with her head in her hand gesturing to Mike.

"Oh yeah, what was the name of it?" I asked.

"Some Steven Segal movie...he was fucking them cats up man," she said smiling, showing her gold tooth.

"Damn your breath stinks!" Gabby said getting up from the table.

"Fuck you bitch. Your ass stinks. Silly ass," Dana said. I didn't smell her breath at all; I think Gabby just didn't like Dana. She took every opportunity to insult her and they would always get into arguments. I decided to change the subject.

"How's business Jon?" I said turning to him.

"Cool. Shit is pretty steady. You know that was a good idea Nate had giving some of our business to the Latin Kings and Vice Lords until things cool off. They have been making a little extra and they feel better about Nate because of it," Jon said eating his cantaloupe.

"You know that's never been done before, sharing your business with rivals," Pete said.

"They are our allies Pete; we trust them. Plus the intelligence I put on their asses checked out!" I said smiling. Everyone chuckled and we finished our breakfast.

At our meeting, I laid out our next move. I received a call from one of our intelligence sources who happened to be a downtown court clerk that our trial date would definitely be in November, which gave us about four months to maneuver. If all went according to plan, Nate would never get to trial.

"Ok, we are set for November, so we have to act fast, but we have to move with precision," I instructed. I proceeded to go over every move, how it should be done and when. I made everyone repeat their roles back to me. I had to leave nothing to chance. We adjourned the meeting and went to work.


## ORLAND HILLS MALL TWO WEEKS LATER...

"Will you be paying by cash or credit card, ma'am?" the store clerk asked.

"Credit Card and can you place the receipt in the bag for me please?" the young woman asked.

"Sure. When are you due?" the clerk asked.

"I'm due on October 17th, and it can't come fast enough!" the young woman said smiling.

"Know what you are having yet?" the clerk inquired.

"Nah, I want to be surprised," the woman answered. The two exchanged laughs and departed. As the young woman walked into the parking lot toward her car, she heard the loud crash of an obvious car accident. The occupants of the vehicles immediately got out of their cars and started screaming at each other causing a scene that everyone including the young woman stopped to watch. Then a black van pulled up behind her quietly. A man got out of the van and grabbed the pregnant woman, and in one quick motion picked her up and put her into the van as another man got out of the driver's side, picked up the keys to the car from the ground, got in and drove off.

## NEW LENOX:

"Phase one done...," the voice over the phone said plainly.

"Good, did anyone see you?" I asked.

"Nah, I don't think so. The accident worked perfectly," the voice said.

"Good take her to the designated place and wait for Dana to get there. Remember don't harm her in any way," I instructed.

"You got it," the voice said.

"Ok," looking at Nate. "Phase one is done. Dana go to the safe house and do as we talked about, but be careful not to hurt her in any way. Make sure you send someone out to get her whatever she wants to eat or drink," I said.

"Cool," Dana said as she picked up all of the equipment to load into the truck.

## ONE HOUR LATER AT NORTHWESTERN HOSPITAL...

"Dr. McFadden, your daughter called. She is meeting with her fiancé and staying with him for the night to talk. She will call you tonight when you get home," the receptionist said.          "Ok, I'm going to be here late anyway. Thanks Lillian."

As the receptionist left the room, Dr. McFadden started to pick up the dictaphone and started to read his next set of films when there was a knock on the door.

"Come in," he said.

"Dr. McFadden, I'm sorry to disturb you, but we have a new cleaning person today. His name is Dante and I will be showing him where to clean in the room here."

"Oh, no problem. Nice to meet you Dante, good luck with your new position," the doctor said casually.

Later during cleaning the young man placed a video cassette into Dr. McFadden's bag and left the room. Later that night McFadden drove home with the police escort behind him in an unmarked car. As he pulled into the parking area of his condo he rolled his window down and spoke to the officer.

"I will be ok from here. Thanks. I will see you tomorrow," the doctor said.

"Are you sure? I could walk you up and check everything out sir," the officer said.

"Nah, I think things will be ok," he responded.

"You have a good night," the officer shot back and drove off.

The doctor was tired of living with security and police. He just wanted the whole thing to be over. As he walked into his home, he threw the keys to the car on the table and laid his bag down. He wiped his head, yawned and gave a long stretch. He checked his messages and heard the usual. The condo was adorned with rich and costly paintings and Victorian furniture. There were pictures of him, his daughter and the deceased mother on the tables, along with pictures of him with other doctors and dignitaries. He undid his tie and picked his bag up and went into the bedroom. When he tossed the bag onto the bed a videotape peeked out. *What the hell is this*, he thought. He pulled the tape out. There was masking tape on the front and someone had written "play me" in crayon. The doctor walked to his study bewildered about the tape and feeling a bit spooked. He turned the television on and placed the video tape into the recorder and hit play. He turned on a desk light and put on his glasses to view the tape.

He saw his daughter completely naked lying on a bed that was covered in plastic. She was blindfolded with her legs were stretched open and her arms tied down to the bed. Her mouth was gagged. He jumped in horror and started toward the phone when a voice spoke to him from out of the shadows.

"I wouldn't do that if I were you," Pete said sitting down with three mafia guys standing by him.

"Who the hell are you and what have you done with my daughter, you punk?" the doctor said angrily.

"Now doc, I am here to help you. You need to relax and put the phone down," Pete said calmly.

"I'm calling the police you son-of-a-bitch," the doctor yelled.

"If you call the police, she will die tonight. That's a guarantee," Pete said sipping coffee.

The doctor stood for a moment and slammed the phone down seething.

"I want my daughter back tonight!" The doctor gritted his teeth visibly livid.

"And I want you to have her back, but not tonight. I am here to work with you doc. I am the negotiator. I am her to help you get your daughter back in one piece," Pete said calmly.

"This is about that case, isn't it?" the doctor said angrily. Pete just smiled and began to rise out of his chair.

"Doctor, you are involved in a huge case – a case that could send my client to jail for a very long time. We are prepared to offer you your daughter back and one-million dollars cash transferred into an off-shore account of your choice. In return all you have to do is recant your testimony against my client. If not your daughter will be gang raped and murdered along with your unborn grandchild. Those are the terms," Pete said plainly.

"Detective Jackson was right...you *are* murdering dogs," the doctor said angrily as he sat on the couch.

Pete sat next to him.

"Look doc, this is a chance. You better take it. If you don't, they're gonna kill your daughter and grandchild and you know what, people will be murdered and will be getting high anyway. It is unavoidable," Pete reasoned.

The doctor snatched his glasses off and wiped away a tear that was forming in his eye.

"I just want my daughter back. She is all I have left in the world," he said beginning to sob. Then the phone rang. The doctor looked at Pete startled and unsure what to do as the phone entered the third ring.

"You better answer that, but talk on the speaker phone," Pete instructed.

"Hello?" The doctor tried to sound calm.

"Yes, Doctor McFadden this is Detective Jackson. I am sorry to bother you so late. I heard you sent the officer home tonight is everything ok?" she said through the speakerphone.

"Oh....yes. I just wanted to be alone tonight. I had a rough night at the hospital and I am very tired, that's all."

"I understand.....it took you a while to answer the phone. Were you asleep?" Jackson asked.

"No, just getting out of the shower and I heard the phone ring."

"Well ok...I won't keep you then. I guess I will see you Friday morning ok?" Jackson said.

"Yes ma'am, I'll see you then," the doctor said before hitting the button and killing the call.

"Good job doc! I even almost believed you," Pete said. "Well doc, I've got to call my client. Will this be a deal or a funeral?"

The doctor leaned over and reflected on his daughter and her safety.

"A deal," he said softly.

"Good man, now you have a meeting Friday with Jackson and the grand jury, that's when you will change the story. Just tell them you're not sure who you saw and that evening you will get your daughter back *and* become one-million dollars richer," Pete said.

"I don't give a damn about the money; I just want my daughter back. And someday you animals will get what you deserve!" The doctor scowled at Pete.

"Don't try anything funny, doctor. We will be watching you all the time. By Saturday this will be all over. Oh and just in case you decide to take our money and flip on us think about this; we got to you once. We will get to you again," Pete said emphatically. He pulled out his phone and called the house in New Lenox, and gave G the signal that they had a deal. "Single mother head of household". Pete said plainly.

"Good now get the hell out of there and get here. Remember don't touch anything and make sure the guys keep their gloves on," I said on the other end. That part was finally over.

We had to wait to see what the doctor would do. Since we heard he really didn't want to get involved in the first place, my hunch was he would follow suit.

"What's going on?" Nate asked.

"Nothing. So far everything is going fine. The doctor seems willing to do whatever it takes to get his daughter back," I replied.

"Good, I don't want to kill that bitch G, but you know I would if that fucker flips on us," Nate said drinking a bottle of beer.

"I know Nate. I think everything will be ok and it won't have to come to that," I said trying to calm him.

Nate's freedom was important to all of us, but killing a pregnant woman and her unborn child was barbaric to me. I wanted no part of that on me, so I prayed this doctor would just play along. Nate and the rest of them were out of control and I knew Nate would kill that woman in a minute and Dana would kill her even faster. Dana and her people were keeping the young girl tied up but were feeding her and treating her pretty well. It was imperative that she stayed blindfolded though. We couldn't take any chances of her identifying any of us.

"How's Gabriella and the baby? Everything ok?" I asked Nate trying to change the subject.

"Cool. I felt the baby kick last night man it was incredible," Nate said glowing.

"When do you all find out what sex the baby is?"

"Next month. I have been trying to keep Gabby as unaware as possible about what is going on. We are gonna get married after all of this is over. She said we will have a big ceremony after the baby is born, when she gets her body back," Nate said smiling.

"I hear you. Look Nate everything is gonna work out fine, just let me handle things ok?"

"No problem G, I trust you. It's just that the people we are dealing with. You know, I don't think they understand the magnitude of the situation. You know what I am saying? Their inexperience scares me a little."

"Yeah, I know but we gotta work with what we have man...just make the best of it," I explained. Nate picked up his beer bottle and turned to look out of the window.


## FRIDAY MORNING CHICAGO POLICE HEADQUARTERS:

"Hey Jackie, do you want the diet or the regular?" asked Detective Jackson's partner.

"The diet," she replied starring out of the window.

"You know we haven't heard anything from your guy, what is his name….Pookie?"

"You know I was just thinking about him also. It's been about two weeks."

"You want me to send a couple of guys out to check on his whereabouts?"

"No, unless I am very wrong my hunch is he is already dead."

"I hope not Jackie, but if so there must be a body somewhere. I think we should really get some guys on the street to…," The detective said before Jackson cut him off.

"You won't find a body, no one will. The more I delve into this case, the more I get the feeling I am fighting more than Nathan Williams. I get the feeling there's something deeper, something more sinister going on you know?"

Then an officer gave a gentle knock on the office door before he opened it.

"Detective Jackson, Dr. McFadden is here," the officer said.

"Good, show him in," she said as she bit into her sandwich.

The two detectives quickly prepared the table where the doctor would sit and wiped their mouths.

Detective Jackson cleaned her hands with sanitizer and adjusted her blouse.

"Dr. McFadden, how are you? Did you get the call from the officer this morning?" Jackson's partner asked. Jackson came from around her desk and extended her hand for the doctor to shake. "Everything is going to work out fine. The most important thing is to be calm and relax. Now I have talked to the DA and with your testimony, as well as some other information we have gathered, this should go fairly smooth." Jackson noticed the doctor's unsettled demeanor. As the doctor sat down he looked around and wringed his hands together looking a bit antsy. "You ok? Doctor can I get you anything?" Jackson asked.

"No, I'm fine. I'm just a little nervous...I will be glad when this is all over. There's something I wanted to talk to you about detective, I...," the doctor said before Jackson cut in.

"Hold your point doctor. I don't want to cut you off, but we need to go over your testimony a bit. The prosecution will be here momentarily and I want you to be relaxed and just listen to what he says ok?" Jackson said.

As Jackson talked to him her partner noticed the nervous body language he exhibited. The attorney for the prosecution walked in while Jackson was prepping the doctor. Everyone exchanged pleasantries and they started to get down to business.

"Now doctor, what is vitally important here is not only what you say, but how you say it. Try not to use words or phrases like "I think" or "Maybe" and "Probably". Their lawyer will try to make you nervous, and trip you up. He may even yell at you a little, but don't worry. We won't let him bark at you too much. Now we are going to do a little role playing ok? I will be their lawyer throwing some questions at you and you just be yourself.   Relax and answer them, ok?" The attorney coached. After going over several questions and answers the lawyer finally got to the question most important. "Now Doctor, are you sure my client, Nathan Williams, was the one you saw at the park that day, straddled over the deceased?"

"Well, I....I'm not sure."   The doctor said nervously, knowing what his response would bring.

"Uh, no doctor that's where you say 'Yes, he was' like we talked about, remember?"  the lawyer said with a half smile.

"But I am not so sure.....all these kids look alike you know what I mean.  I have to be sure, I don't want to send this guy to jail if I am not sure...I'm just not really certain," the doctor stammered.

"Look doctor I understand your nervousness, but this is very important.  Now you told Detective Jackson you were sure; you gave a statement; and signed it.  Now let's just focus and try again ok?"  The lawyer said firmly sitting on the side of the desk.

"I know what I said, and I know what I signed, I'm just not really sure right now.  I could be mistaken."  The doctor looked at the three of them.  The attorney glared at Detective Jackson, and shot up from the desk stuffing papers into his attaché case.

"What do you mean you don't know, you're not sure?  What are you trying to pull here doctor?" Jackson asked agitated.  Then the doctor's lawyer walked into the office.

"Sorry I'm late Paulie...damned traffic was horrendous!"

"Well it's good that you could join us sir, because your client here is about to derail this whole case! He's got a shot of the nerves and now he's changing his whole testimony!" Jackson said angrily.

"I talked with my client last night. h

He says he's not sure of what he saw. Now he's entitled to do that detective, we don't want to send an innocent man to jail for murder!" Dr. McFadden's lawyer stated.

The prosecutor walked toward the door and summoned Jackson to speak to him in the hallway. As Jackson walked into the hallway her partner started to question the doctor and the lawyer.

"Diane, you better get that guy up to speed. We are going up against one of the best defense attorneys in the state; and my office isn't going in there with "maybe", "I don't know", and "I'm not sure". Get that guy up to speed detective or we will drop the charges. We have no other choice," the lawyer warned.

"Look, I've got other things. Just give me a little time," Jackson said.

"What about the info you got from the guy on the inside with them, the guy talking about the drugs. Where is he?"

"Well....we haven't heard from him, we fear he may have been murdered."

"He may be dead!!! Call me by Monday, detective, so I can call the judge." The lawyer walked away. Jackson then stormed into the office, walked around to her desk, and stood with her arms folded glaring at the doctor.

"Who got to you?" Jackson asked.

"Got to me? No one. It's not like that detective, I'm simply not sure that's all."

"That's bullshit and you know it. Someone got to you doctor, now who was it?" Jackson demanded. The doctor fell silent.

"You know if you're on the take for these fucking guys doctor...," Jackson's partner said before the doctor's lawyer chimed in.

"Now you question my client's integrity? Don't answer that Paul," the lawyer said.

"Do you know what's at stake here doctor? Do you have any fucking idea what the state and I have put into this damn case, huh?" Jackson questioned firmly.

"Maybe what's at stake here is your professional reputation. You want my client to lie to protect...," McFadden's lawyer interrupted.

"Shut up mouthpiece!" Jackson yelled. Jackson stood there with her hands on her hips glaring.

"Both of you get the fuck out!" Jackson gritted teeth.

"You'll be hearing from my office detective!" The lawyer shouted as they left the office. After they walked out Detective Jackson went into a fit of rage.

"Fuck!" She screamed as she threw all of the papers and items off of her desk and flipped it over. Her partner looked at her and bowed his head. They knew their case was over. Then an officer opened the door after hearing the commotion.

"What the fuck do you want?" Jackson yelled.

"They got your son downstairs, their booking him." The officer looked around at the mess in the office.

"Booking him for what?" Jackson asked incredulously.

"Possession with intent."

Jackson pushed past her partner and the officer scurrying downstairs to the booking area. After Jackson left, her partner started cleaning up the mess and picking up Jackson's desk.

"How's things going buddy?" The officer walked over to Jackson's partner.

"Shit this case is unraveling more and more by the minute."

"Yeah, that's what I wanted to talk to you about." The officer said gently closing the door for privacy.

## DOWNSTAIRS IN BOOKING:

"What the hell are you doing?" Jackson asked looking at her son sitting handcuffed to a desk and answering questions.

"Look detective the arresting officers say they found close to two pounds of marijuana in his car and a couple of joints on his person so...," the sergeant said.

"That's bullshit, let me call a lawyer and...," Jackson fumed.

"Detective you know the situation. Call whoever you want, but he's gonna be booked and arraigned in the morning. I'm just following protocol."

Over the next few hours, Detective Jackson raised her son's bail money, and spoke with him about how he may have been framed with the drugs planted on him. After getting him home, Jackson went back to her office at police headquarters looked around in despair, and slammed herself down in her chair. *How did everything go so wrong so fast? Who got to the doctor? Who planted the drugs?* She knew Nathan had something to do with it all, but how was she going to prove it? She knew she had been outsmarted and outfoxed. Waves of emotion and anger swept over her as she placed her head down on her desk. Everyone had left her office area, and she could hear the cleaning crew coming in. *How could it have happened, and how was it going to be explained to Inspector Trent?*

It was only a matter of time before the local press heard about her son being booked on felony possession with intent, and she pondered how she would handle the embarrassment of that. She had poured her soul into this case only for it to end in shame, embarrassment and a victory for Nathan Williams. While her head was on the desk she could smell the smoke of a cigar and a presence watching her, she jerked her head up and it was Inspector Trent standing in the doorway with his arms folded leaning against the door jam.

"My first case as a detective was this serial rapist on the south side, real slippery bastard you know. This asshole was accused of raping close to seven women in the Roseland area, but no one could ever catch him. Most of the women he raped were prostitutes and all we had in the way of a description was a bullshit composite sketch, and you know how fucked up those can be." He leaned on the door jam and continued. "So my partner and I spent the next six months chasing bullshit leads, getting half-ass information on the street before we caught a break. We got an anonymous call that he was hiding out somewhere in the Chatham area. We never found out who made the call, but we checked it out anyway. Come to find out it was true. The asshole was hiding in some broad's apartment. So we get his warrant info and everything, hi-tail our asses over to the apartment building. My partner and I grab his ass up and take him to the precinct; book him; get a few of the girls to testify it was him and all; and we feel we have an open and shut case, right? Wrong. Come to find out this fucker fled the country to Uganda and has an identical twin he left behind here in the States. We got the wrong fucking brother!" Trent said half smiling and shaking his head. As Jackson sat looking at him wondering why he was telling his story he gives her the moral. "I learned a valuable lesson that day: never celebrate until you have a conviction!" Trent said reflecting.

"Why didn't they just find him in Africa and extradite his ass back here?" Jackson asked bewildered.

"Who the fuck is gonna spend that kind of taxpayer money to go half way around the world to bring back a guy accused of raping a bunch of black prostitutes, in the 70's no less? Nah, we got our asses cleaned on that one. You know why? Cause the fucker outsmarted us that's why. That's what happened to you Jackie. Nathan Williams outsmarted you just like I predicted he would," Trent said with a smirk.

"He's just another street punk," Jackson retorted.

"No he ain't just another street punk. This guy is a demon; he's an enigma wrapped up in a riddle! And you don't have what it takes to collar him!" Trent barked. "Now I'm shipping your ass to Lincoln Park. Maybe you can handle that kind of atmosphere, but you're done here. Your transfer papers are all set and ready to go." Trent turned to walk out of the doorway when Jackson said, "It ain't over top. I can't let him get away with what he has done!"

"He already has Jackie, let it go. We'll get some other guys on him, but we live to fight another day, it's over...I'm warning you! Let it go!" Trent yelled.

Jackson sat staring out of the doorway as tears rolled down her cheeks, completely engulfed in anger.


## ONE WEEK LATER IN NEW LENOX...

A week or so after the prosecution dropped the case and cut Nate loose, he made me put together a party. He was celebrating his freedom, so he just didn't want any kind of party, he made me go all out. He invited all of his people: all of the top gangsters in Chicago that were our allies, even some of the freelancers. He had prostitutes flown in from Vegas, and lobster and crab flown in from the east coast. There was caviar and about four thousand dollars worth of alcohol including approximately fifty bottles of Cristal champagne. Thousands of dollars of food catered from the best restaurants in downtown Chicago; a professional DJ was also flown in from New York for the festivities; and to top it all off Nate made it all mandatory black tie! Hugo sent Nate and I a box of Havana cigars each along with congratulatory notes. I remember Dana asking about the cigars and wondering how Hugo got Cuban cigars through customs to us.

"Oh, you think this motherfucker knows how to ship cocaine around the globe, but is dumbfounded as to how to ship cigars?" Nate asked her as we all laughed.

Anyone that was someone in the criminal world was there. Everyone that was walking away from us when we were in trouble wanted to share in the celebration. You see things were loosening up now, now guys were free to make their profits without worrying about what was gonna happen to Nate. Defeating the Chicago Police and the DA gave the "family" that much more street credibility as the top drug family in city. As our allies and "friends" celebrated, our enemies worried. You see while we were in trouble with the cops some of them took advantage cause they knew we really couldn't fight back. We had suffered shakedowns, some of our freelancers were robbed and even murdered. Even some of the mafia guys got smoked by some of our enemies. Now that we were free and had won, everybody knew certain people were gonna get clipped.

"Everybody stand up, I wanna propose a toast to the baddest motherfucker this side of the Mississippi, King Nate!" a young man said admiringly. Everyone stood up and clanged bottles and glasses and clapped their hands in joy and admiration as Nate stood up raising a bottle of Cristal in the air as he received his praise. Nate was the new king of crime in Chicago.

The next morning I remember having a colossal headache – champagne has always had that effect on me. After washing up I remember walking downstairs into the kitchen and seeing Gabriella at the kitchen table eating ice cream and a bologna sandwich!

"How can you eat that shit this early in the morning?" I asked. She didn't even look up as she gave me the finger. I smiled as I opened the refrigerator. The house seemed quiet to me. "Hey where is everybody?" I asked Gabby.

"Your brother, Mike, and Jon went to some meeting."

"What about Dana and Pete?"

"Gone to make a pickup." She was flipping through a magazine.

"So it's just you and I, huh?"

"Wrong…I'm going shopping," she said as she stuffed the rest of her sandwich into her mouth.

"Take some guys with you," I instructed. Gabby was getting close to her due date and the closer she got, the more anti-sociable and moody she became. As some of the mafia guys came in from doing the grocery shopping, I looked out of the window into the massive side yard to see Nate's two devil dogs: Cleopatra and Nefertiti just sitting and staring at me through the window almost without blinking. *Damn they give me the creeps*, I thought.

## HYDE PARK

"Hello Jackie, can I come in?" Jackson's partner asked in her doorway.

"Sure Donnie, come in. Can I get you something; coffee or anything?" Jackson offered.

"Nah I had some before I came over. What did you want to talk to me about?"

"I guess you know I got transferred up north, huh?" Jackson asked as she stuffed her hands into the back pockets of her cutoff jeans.

"Yeah, Jackie I'm sorry. I really am. Hey how's your boy doing? Did he beat the case?"

"No. The prosecution gave him a urine test and he pissed hot. They gave him five years probation. He checked himself into a program ordered by the state, but he's coming around."

"Hey look Jackie keep your head up, you're a damn good detective. You're the only detective that has ever had the guts to investigate that guy and bring in an arrest. That's huge."

"Yeah, but no conviction, I didn't collar him Donnie. We are evaluated by collars, not arrests you know that."

"Well you may get another chance one day, you never know."

"That's what I wanted to talk to you about. I've got some leads and I think with a little patience this time I can get him."

"Count me out."

"Why? I thought you were my friend...my partner?"

"Jackie you know this has nothing to do with how I feel about you, but you're off the case; you're transferred. Let it go, move on. Now this guy Nathan I...I just got bad feelings about him, and I have to think about my career...my family."

"What about mine? Look what this fucker did to *my career and my family!*"

The young man looked at her sorrowfully, then grabbed her by the hand and guided her down on the couch to talk to her.

"Jackie, listen to me, the day they booked your son, this patrolman talked to me and warned me to stay away from Nathan Williams. He told me I didn't know what I was involved in, and it would behoove me and you to go easy and get off the case or something bad might happen," the young detective said quietly.

"Right; the patrolman that initially told me about the booking after I got pissed at McFadden. I remember him! What is his name?"

"Dammit Jackie he has no name, he's a phantom...a spook. He exists, but he doesn't exist! What do you think? You're just gonna roll downtown and ask him, and he's gonna tell you who he is, who he's connected to and what he knows? Forget it! Now somebody's behind Nathan, there's something else, something deeper, you said it yourself. And I don't want to get involved!"

"Everybody's so fucking afraid of this thug; he ain't shit Donnie! He sent that cop in there; he planted those drugs on my son; and he got the doctor to change his story. You know that?" Jackson yelled.

The young detective took a deep breath and spoke.

"Ok Jackie I'm gonna ask you a few questions, and if you can give me some reasonable answers I will go back on the case with you, but if you can't I don't ever want to talk to you about Nathan Williams again. Deal?"

"Deal." Jackson replied defiantly with her hands on her hips.

"Who is it that makes sure that no judge ever signs a search warrant to search that massive ass compound he lives in New Lenox? Why is it that no matter how much evidence you come up with neither Trent nor any of his superiors will ever allow you to place Nathan under surveillance of any kind? Why have all of the notes and interrogation tapes we had on Nathan when we arrested him been destroyed or have disappeared? Why is it that Nathan is believed to be involved directly or indirectly in over twenty-five murders in the Chicago land area and no cop: local, state, or federal has ever questioned him on anything? Why is it that Nathan Williams lives in a two-million dollar mansion with a plethora of ex-cons, and owns at least ten to fifteen businesses across this fucking county with only a high school education, and the last known job this guy has on record is McDonald's? And here's a free little tidbit Jackie: Nathan's brother Derrick...his mom was a hopeless junkie, a nomad of a woman who was on the verge of losing Derrick at the time of her death, which came by overdose, I might add. All of that information was on file at DCFS three years ago. I checked the files again at DCFS a month ago and all of those files have been destroyed. Who has the power to cover all of that up Jackie? Who has the power to do all of this and why are they doing it? You're sadly mistaken Jackie. There is a cloud of evil that surrounds that guy, and I don't want to get involved with him anymore."

Having said that, the young detective started toward the door. As he turned to look back, he saw that Detective Jackson had her head down and arms folded.

"Jackie you've had a decent career, don't ruin it on this witch hunt. Nathan Williams will get what's coming to him, his kind always does," the young detective said. After the young man walked out of the door, Jackson sat on the plush couch and started to cry. She felt used and defeated, and she knew that her career was virtually ruined. She would go on being a detective, but few in her field would take her seriously. Life was so unfair! How a man like this can get away with what he has, and if he was being protected as her partner claimed, who was behind it? Soon her sorrow turned to rage and hate. Nathan Williams was a murdering drug dealer. That was without a doubt, but she was going to find out who was protecting him at any cost.

Later that night Nate announced a meeting and wanted all of us there.

"Did you hear that motherfucker talking shit, trying to kiss my ass, Mike? Calling me the baddest nigga near the Mississippi. Like I don't know he cuffed nearly twenty thousand from me last quarter. Dana, make him the first motherfucker you murder. You got that?" Nate snarled sitting at his desk with his feet up.

"Understood." Dana said while eating a banana.

"Alright listen up, this is important. It seems that our old friend Titus has surfaced near Calumet City. What do you have, Jimmy?" Nate said turning to the informant to give him the floor.

"Well he's been on the lam obviously...turns out he was in Detroit all of this time. A couple of the Gangster Disciples smuggled him back here about a month ago; he's staying with some broad in Calumet City. He only comes out to get a haircut every other week or so usually at about three in the morning, and to see his kid in Harvey. The barbershop he goes to is the one in Dolton, owned by you guys. We've been watching him go back and forth for about three weeks now," the informant said.

"Good that's where I want him at," Nate said flatly.

"Nate, that's too risky. Titus will have City, County, and State police looking for him, probably the FBI, too," I warned.

"Then we'll kill him before they find him," Nate said smiling.

"You know Nate, G might be right. Maybe we should look at an alternative plan...maybe one where we tip off the police as to his whereabouts or something. This kill might be a little too risky for us, plus you know they're still probably watching our asses, too," Mike said.

"Fuck that shit. I been waiting for years for this motherfucker and now I got him where I want him. I'm killing his ass and you all ain't talking me out of it, so don't try. Now I'm open to any and all plans of killing him, but he's gonna die!" Nate insisted.

"When are you talking about doing this exactly?" Pete asked.

"Soon. I'm going to settle all accounts with them fucking gangbangers on the west side and the fucking freelancers that shit on us during our trouble with the police. That bitch Detective Jackson and a few others are going to get dealt with too. I'm settling all accounts, you better believe that shit. There's gonna be a cry from the criminal world that you won't believe, but for now I'm gonna wait. After my baby is born, I'm gonna shut all of those fuckers down!" Nate said deep in thought.

# CHAPTER 4

## POSSESSED

Nate wanted to take over. He wanted to control all of the drug sales in the city of Chicago. Jon had washed about sixty percent of our drug revenues in so-called "businesses" around the city and suburbs. The registered owners of these fronts were paid informants and "associates" of the "family", but they knew if so much as a nickel of the profits were stolen watch out! But you know how it goes, there's always some wise ass who will try the system – idiots like Catfish Lenny.

Lenny was a guy we knew from the block back in the old days. He was never one of our running buddies, but he was cool. So when we needed fronts for businesses we turned him on. Now with this guy all he had to do was manage a club we had on the southeast side near Exchange Street. Mike provided security from his regime for the place. All Lenny had to do was keep things quiet and get paid. But when Nate got into legal trouble, he like many others thought Nate would go down, so Lenny started skimming from the profits. When some of the guys we had in there started warning him about it, he said, 'Fuck Nate! Shit I hear his ass might be in jail soon anyway. I'm looking out for me!' This dummy skimmed well over twenty-thousand dollars from the club in a little over three months! Needless to say, once Nate beat the case, Lenny had to cover his tracks and kiss Nate's ass for a little insurance. That's when he made that ridiculous statement at Nate's party, 'Everybody stand up for the baddest motherfucker this side of the Mississippi!' But it was too late. Nate had already given instructions to Dana to make him the first on the list to be murdered.

"Open the door fool, it's Dana,"

"Oh, hey what's up Dana? I didn't expect you until next week. How's Nate and G?" Lenny asked.

"They all good...you got something to eat in here I'm hungry as hell!" Dana said.

"Yeah, look in the kitchen. I think it's some leftover chicken in there, help yourself. Did I ever introduce you to my fiancée, Dana?" Lenny asked.

"No I don't think so, I'm Dana...nice to meet you." She said in between bites of chicken.

"Nice to meet you also; I'm Shaunda," the young woman said extending her hand. But Dana didn't extend hers, she just smiled and kept chewing.

"These are just some of the guys I roll with, don't mind them," Dana said referring to the five mafia men.

"All this new furniture around this fucking place Lenny? What did you do, hit the lottery or some shit?" Dana asked jokingly.

"Nah the place needed a little fixing up, you like it?" Lenny asked nervously.

Dana just stared at him without batting an eye. Now Lenny was really nervous.

"Where's that twenty-five thousand at nigga?" Dana was wiping her hands and mouth glaring at him.

"What are you talking about Dana. I ain't got no twenty-five thousand dollars?" Lenny was nearly white with fear. Dana motioned to her men.

"Take this motherfucker in the back and murder his ass; ya'll know what to do!" Dana instructed. One of the mafia guys knocked Lenny to the floor and they dragged him to the back of the apartment as he kicked and screamed. Upon witnessing this, his fiancée started screaming for them to stop and started toward the men in Lenny's defense.

"Bitch, sit your ass down and shut the fuck up!" Dana said drawing her gun.

"Dana don't do this please, not in front of my woman, please Dana....Please!" Lenny begged through tears and sorrow.

"Nigga fuck you. You should have thought about that shit when you was stealing our fucking money! You and this bitch living it up on our cash!" Dana said as she motioned for the guys to take him in the back, this time more emphatically. As the guys took Lenny to the back of the apartment and closed the door Dana picked up the young woman's purse and took all of her identification out and put it into her pocket. As she heard Lenny's screams from the back of the apartment, she started getting hysterical and crying profusely. "Look whore don't piss me off; I told you to shut the fuck up!" Dana said as she cocked her pistol and pointed it directly in front of her face. The woman flopped down on the couch and placed her hands over her ears in an attempt to stifle the screams of her lover. There were shots fired from what sounded like a silencer. Dana just looked at the woman and smiled. After about fifteen minutes, one of the mafia guys came out of the door with blood streaming down the front of his clothes and whispered in Dana's ear. When the young woman saw this she fainted. The other guys came out with blood on their clothes, also. "Are we good yet?" Dana asked.

"Yeah, it's done," one of the guys answered.

"Alright let's get the fuck out of here. But wipe this place down first," Dana instructed.

"Ok, but what do you want to do with her?" One of the guys asked while motioning to the fainted woman.

"I don't give a shit.  Do that thing ya'll do, but be back downstairs in twenty.  I got a stop to make," Dana said as she walked out of the door.

When the police arrived the next day they found a gruesome sight.  The young woman was sprawled on the floor with her clothes ripped apart and had been savagely raped and beaten, with two shots to her chest.  They also found the bloody body of Lenny on the bathroom floor with the head sawed away from the body.  One of the detectives found the beaten and mangled head of Lenny in the toilet.  Needless to say, later that night the grisly discovery was all over the local news.  As Nate, Gabriella and I watched, Dana came in smiling with take-out from a local restaurant.

"Who would do something sick like that?" Gabriella said.

"I don't know, that's horrible," I said glaring at Nate.  After Gabby got up to hobble to the bathroom – now due any day – I confronted Nate.  "You know you gotta tell her to chill with some of these killings.  This shit is like a horror show or something.  Every damn night Nate?  Enough is enough already!" I said in a loud whisper.  I looked over at Dana and she was smiling while drinking a V8.

Nate wanted to get Titus at the barbershop which he frequented in the middle of the night; he figured it would be the best way since no one would be around to see much.  Also, since the shop was owned by the family, we could get our guy to pretty much cover for us and make the whole thing happen…it was a perfect plan.  So when the barber came over to give Nate his usual haircut he started setting everything up.

"What's up Oscar?  How has shit been for you?" Nate asked.

"It's been cool Nate, just cutting hair as usual." The young barber answered as he gave Nate the mirror.

"Looking good man, but take a little more off the top this time for me," Nate answered as he gave him the mirror back.

"So I hear that punk-ass Titus has been getting his hair cut there in the middle of the night, huh?" Nate said holding his head down for the young barber.

"Yeah man, he's been sneaking his ass up there with a couple of his guys you know? I really wish he would just go some where else," the barber lamented.

"Well you know that's what I wanted to talk to you about; I was hoping you could help a brother out and let us do a job."

"Cool, whatever man, just tell me what it is."

"Good, I want to use the shop to clip his ass next month."

The young man paused a little and quickly continued his shaping.

"Uh, I don't know Nate. I don't know if I want something like that done in my shop, man." The barber said cautiously. With that, Nate's eyes bulged as he stood up and whirled around and gave the barber a fist to the jaw in one quick motion. Everyone stood up in surprise, as Dana spit out her drink in laughter.

"That ain't your fucking shop, bitch. That's my damn shop, and if I say we drop a motherfucker in there, that's what the fuck is gonna happen!" Nate growled.

"Be cool man. Come on man get up," Dana said laughing at the young man. I just shook my head – another fiasco, but I was worried about what the guy would do in retrospect.

"Get your punk-ass up and finish my shit, and if you nick me, I'll stick your ass in a fucking hole," Nate shouted.　I felt so bad for the guy.　I noticed he was shaking, and was fighting back tears.

Later, as usual I approached Nate about the incident. This was a sticky situation because I heard through my contacts that Oscar would probably run to the authorities if he had been muscled, plus this guy was a straight arrow.　The police would probably believe him because of it.

"Nate what were you thinking?　You can't just pummel the guy for no reason like that.　He's probably gonna run to the District Attorney's office," I reasoned.

"Fuck the DA!　That motherfucker didn't get the loan for that shop from the DA's office he got it from me!" Nate said.

"Nate, the guy is a straight arrow.　You can't just muscle him, maybe you should've just finessed him a little…"

"Finesse my ass!　That motherfucker is gonna do as he is told or he will end up in the Cal Sag river!　You know G, the more I talk to you, I get the feeling that you don't understand what we are trying to do here.　Do you understand?" he asked mockingly.

"Yeah I understand, I understand," I replied.

"I don't think you do; I don't think you understand. We are trying to build a criminal organization here, a drug organization!　And you can't do that passing out bibles and flowers, G.　Sometimes you gotta kick a little ass to get things going out there!" Nate said.

"Nate you miss the whole point.　This guy could have had a wire on; he still may go to the DA or maybe the FBI.　We can't afford another indictment Nate," I reasoned.

"G, you're my brother and I love you, but you need to grow some balls my friend.　You're a little paranoid.　In fact that's your area, find out about this guy. Get me some info instead of always trying to tell me how to do my job," Nate said.

I didn't say anything, it wouldn't have mattered anyway. He didn't care, he just didn't care. Later that night, we all sat down and mapped out a strategy for killing Titus.

"How's our doctor friend doing, G?" Jon asked.

"He's cool. He opened a private practice in Bermuda; his daughter had a little girl; and their living it up on the money they got from us. He's cool, he'll be quiet I think." I said.

"I still can't believe you gave him one million for changing his story Nate," Pete said.

"Are you crazy? I gave him half a million. The other five-hundred thousand was counterfeit," Nate confessed.

"What if he finds out we juked him, and he goes to the police?" Jon asked.

"Who the fuck knows the difference in real bills and fakes in Bermuda? Hell half the time I can't tell the difference," Nate said smiling.

"Somebody needs to make a beer run," Dana said.

"Later, let's do business. Jon, Pete how's shit going?" Nate asked.

"Cool, we need some more surgical masks in the make room. We're starting to run out. We caught a guy cuffing a little rock last week; Mike took care of it though. I talked to Hugo's people yesterday. They are sending the shipment one week late. They ran into a little exporting delay, can we make the trip a week later?" Pete asked.

"I guess so. G get some guys on that run as soon as possible. I'm gonna contact Hugo directly tomorrow. Anything else?" Nate asked.

"Not from me; everything else is peaches and cream," Pete said.

"Jon?" Nate said looking at Jon for his report.

"We got close to fifty million in the money room and about one million on the street. I opened a new currency exchange on the west side per your request. Now that's two restaurants, a club, and a currency exchange, you're all set with that. Everybody got their checks last week, and all of the lawyers are paid in full. Oh, Mike needs a loan from the family is that ok?" Jon asked as Mike looked at Jon sternly.

"A loan, for what Jon?" I asked.

"As you all know big mamma died last week and Pete and I wanted to give her a nice funeral you know...," Mike said.

"We all heard about that Mike and we all give you two our condolences, we all loved big mamma, but how much are you talking?" Nate asked.

"Uh, about twenty thousand," Mike said tentatively.

"That's all? I don't understand you two coming to us for twenty thousand?" Nate asked incredulously. Jon looked down and gave a sly half smile to himself.

"Uh yeah, we just kinda short right now, that's all," Pete said.

"Short? You two make eighty-thousand dollars a month each, how the hell are you short?" Nate snapped.

"Uh Jon can you give us a minute or so?" I said.

"Yeah, no sweat baby, I understand it's a black thing," Jon said smiling as he picked up his attaché and walked toward the office door.

"Yeah, go take a reefer break or something," Nate replied.

"Asshole," Dana said as Jon left the room.

"Now what the fuck is this shit about Mike? You mean to tell me you two are broke?" Nate asked.

"Naw, not broke man, just a little short right now. You know big mamma dying really came unexpected and shit you know," Mike explained.

"That's bullshit. Have you guys saved anything?" Nate asked.

"Well...yeah. A little something," Mike said sheepishly.

"You know, let me tell you all something. This shit ain't gonna last forever. I mean it can end any day, like tomorrow! So you better put something aside and stop being niggers and blowing all of your money on cars, whores, and gambling. That motherfucker Jon has put so much money aside in offshore accounts, it ain't funny. If it ended tomorrow he and that kid of his is set for life. You guys are making eighty-thousand dollars a month, and don't have enough to bury your grandmother? That's a fucking shame!"

"Nate, man we just...," Pete said trying to interrupt.

"I don't want to hear it Pete! It's bullshit! Eighty-thousand dollars a month ya'll make and you can't bury your grandmother! Mike you blow about half of that at the fucking casinos in Vegas at least twice a month. Thought I didn't know that shit, didn't you? Why haven't you gotten with Jon and asked him to show you all how to wash your money? This asshole sat right there a month ago and told me you two where blowing money and I didn't believe him! Fucking niggers!" Nate said walking toward the wall safe. Nate opened the safe and pulled out a stack of money wrapped in plastic totaling about fifty thousand and threw it at Mike. "Here, go bury big mamma. And that ain't no gift, it's a loan! And I want my fucking money back by the end of the month at credit card interest! Now get the hell out of here! You stay G," Nate said. After everyone left the office Nate was livid. Of course he didn't want to show it full force as to embarrass the guys but......eighty-thousand dollars a month, that's a lot of money to blow! "You believe this shit? These two knuckleheads are blowing that kind of money, that's insane!" Nate said clearly frustrated.

"Yeah, I believe it, I tried to tell you," I said.

"Now don't start that I told you shit G. I mean these guys came up with us in the same hood, what the fuck is wrong with them?" Nate asked pulling out a cigar from his box on the desk.

"Nate you can't expect them to have the knowledge that Jon has about money. These guys are brothers from the hood."

"That's bullshit G, we are from the same hood. That's no excuse." Nate lit up and started puffing on his cigar.

"What about Titus? I thought we were gonna discuss him tonight?" I asked.

"Shit I ain't in the mood now. I'll probably talk about it tomorrow night, we got a little time," Nate said puffing and thinking. "Did you talk to the doctors about Gabby and the baby?"

"Yeah, I got a good gynecologist on call for you and a couple of nurses. I still think you should get it done at a hospital Nate, what if something goes wrong?"

"Fuck that, you know Gabby ain't legal G. Them hospital motherfuckers are gonna want papers filled out and shit. Nah, I'll pay them to come here. And if something goes wrong, then we can rush her out, but she's young and the baby was fine the last time we had a checkup here." Nate twirled his cigar in his mouth. Personally I thought he was taking unnecessary chances, but it's his baby. Nate was very cautious and yet impulsive about things. I just hoped everything would turn out well.

The next night we all sat down to talk about Titus. Nate had been on a secure line half the day talking to Hugo about the shipment and other shit. I was really nervous about the call, because it was so long. I thought the feds could've been listening or something; I guess I was just paranoid. I went to talk to Oscar the barber and smoothed things over about the Nate incident. I advised him in a more subtle way to kind of go along with Nate's plan for the shop. I gave him about fifty grand of my own money to get started over after the Titus thing. I mean the shop was all he had and I was afraid Nate might kill him after the job was done. Nate always felt things ran better with no witnesses.

"Ok, listen up. I talked with Hugo today, and everything is cool with the shipment next week. Dana's gonna be going to the west side for about six months or so after the Titus thing. As a matter of fact, a week or two before the Titus thing, I want her and her people already in place."

"In place for what?"

"We're taking the west side G, right after the Titus thing." Nate said flatly.

I was afraid of that. I knew Nate wanted Titus dead, but I thought he was going after the west side a little prematurely. That was the Gangster Disciple stronghold and upon my intelligence, it is estimated that there are at least a few hundred bangers over there. We were tough, but we were outnumbered significantly.

"I don't know Nate. Maybe we should recruit some more guys; we're outnumbered by a lot over there," Pete said.

"We don't have time," Nate said.

"Yeah, but the numbers...," I tried to reason.

"Fuck the numbers. I don't give a shit about numbers. I want that west side! Now them motherfuckers got paid while we were in legal shit, and I ain't forgot those little skirmishes we had to ignore. They cost me a lot of money for about six months and I ain't letting that shit ride!" Nate shouted. Then the phone rang. Nate picked it up and I heard a frantic voice on the other end. Nate's eyes bulged and started shouting into the phone asking a lot of questions. We were all itching to know what happened. "Les, get your fucking ass over here...now!" Nate yelled into the phone before slamming it down so hard it almost broke in two.

After he hung up he just stood there looking directly at me for about five seconds and proceeded to yell and in one swoop used both of his arms and slid everything off of his desk and flipped it over. We all jumped up from our seats and stood wondering what the hell was going on. Nate stormed toward the office door and told Dana to meet him in the kitchen alone. As it turned out the phone call was pretty bad news. The Gangster Disciples shot up one of Nate's strip clubs in Chicago Heights and killed four of his strippers, the bartender, about six patrons, and wounded about thirty others. They also robbed the club manager Lester and cuffed about forty grand to boot. Now Nate was really pissed. You see it wasn't about the money, forty grand was pocket change to us. The problem was the GD's one upped Nate, and he hated to be one upped by anyone, much less gangbangers. Nate sat in conference with Dana in that kitchen for about two hours, with paper and pen, writing out what he wanted. He essentially declared a war on the west side that Chicago won't soon forget. That night Dana and about seventy of her guys left the compound about three in the morning in trucks with all kinds of hardware toward downtown Chicago. I knew what they were going to do, so I beefed up security around the house and told Nate he had to stay put until his war was over. Dana rented out a high rise under the name of Claudia Stills, and was told to run the war from there. But before anything would be done we had a date with Titus.

Titus was living with one of his baby's mothers in Calumet City; he basically never left the apartment. He had a couple of guys from the GD's go and fetch him whatever he wanted whenever he wanted. He would only leave to go get a haircut twice a month at Oscar's shop, at about four in the morning. My people watched him do this for about two months. Everyone knew law enforcement would be looking for Titus, so no one spoke of his whereabouts. I didn't know what Nate's plan was for the killing; I thought he would have had Dana on it, but with her up north it had to be someone else. I never asked, I really didn't want to know the details. Not too long after our meeting, one day I picked up the paper and there he was on the front page leaning back in a barber's chair with a sheet draped over him soaked in blood. There were all kinds of stories on the street about the killing, but eyewitness reports in the shop were pretty consistent.

~ · ~ · ~ · ~ · ~

At about 4:15 AM Titus walked into the barbershop with a couple of his guys to get his usual haircut. After a brief exchange with Oscar and another barber, Titus sat in the chair waiting to get started. Then four strikingly attractive Latina women lightly tapped on the shop window to get the men's attention. Titus sitting with his back to the window and door as to not be noticed by authorities gave a glance and turned back around.

"You know them broads, man?" he asked Oscar.

"No, but I want to get to know them," he said smiling.

"What do you think man, should we let them in?" the other barber asked.

"I ain't never seen them around here before," one of Titus' men said.

"Fuck them! Don't let them in, shit they could be cops," Titus said as he whirled back around in the chair.

Oscar motioned to his watch, and mouthed that they were closed to the young ladies. One of the girls put her hands together in a praying motion, and mouthed please, and the other one pulled her blouse up and pressed her bare breasts up against the glass of the window.

"Damn did you see that, shit they ain't no cops man," another barber said.

"No shit, I know they fine as hell though," one of Titus' men said.

As the girls pleaded through the window, Oscar looked at Titus for the approval.

"Go ahead, shit it might be fun," Titus said with a half smile.

As Oscar walked toward the window, the girls were smiling with a girlish glee, and fixing their hair and faces in a makeshift fashion.

"What's up girls? We're closed," Oscar said.

Upon opening the door he looked at them and their countenance changed from that of a girlish glee, to bone chilling stares. All of the young women just stared at him frightfully. Oscar put his head down and moved aside to let them in. Sorrow engulfed Oscar's heart because he knew...he now knew who they were, and what they were there to do.    There were four of them in all, all were beautiful to look at and very feminine Latina women, yet athletically built.   Two of them had ponytails, and the other two had movie star-styled haircuts.   The one that bore her breasts came in and told them she needed her neck shaped in a very heavy Spanish accent.   One of the pony-tailed girls gave a sexy wink to one of Oscar's barbers as she put down a large gym bag.   The barber gave an anxious smile as he sat up in the chair.   One of Titus' men noticed the athletically shaped arms of one of the women, and started talking to her.   She said she knew no English, and gave him a sexy smile.   The women had a presence about them of sex and danger, which intrigued the men.   Titus leaned back in the chair now feeling more comfortable with the situation and closed his eyes.

"Hurry up Oscar!   I gotta be outta here soon," he said.

It had started to rain outside and the windows fogged up from the humidity.

"Shit, it's raining already," one of the barbers said getting his station ready for the day.

The woman that needed the neck shape asked which chair she should sit in; Oscar motioned for her to sit in the one directly across from Titus.   One of the pony-tailed women inquired about the restroom and Oscar pointed in that direction.   The woman picked up the gym bag and walked into the women's room as the others picked up magazines and flipped through them.

"So are you from around here?" One of the guys asked the girl in the chair.

"Nah, I from uptown," she said in a heavy Spanish accent.

She engaged in small talk with the barber as everyone relaxed.   Oscar draped a smock around Titus' neck to signal that he was getting started and leaned Titus back in the chair. He then walked slowly toward the back of the shop, opened the rear exit door quietly, and walked out. The two women reading the magazines noticed him leaving and spoke to the girl in the chair in Spanish. Then the other woman came out of the restroom with the gym bag, opened it, pulled out four huge handguns with silencers fastened to the barrels, and quietly passed them to the young ladies sitting down while tucking one into her jeans for herself. It began to thunder outside violently, which distracted the men for the split second that the women needed.

"Let's go Oscar, let's do this shit," Titus said with his eyes still closed.

Two of the girls quickly stood up and popped two slugs apiece into the chests and head of his bodyguards, killing them instantly without making much of a sound. The other barbers stood frozen in fear and surprised as the one that was in the barber chair stood up and motioned for them to be quiet by pressing her index finger to her mouth as she smiled devilishly. As the thunder roared, the women worked fast with precision putting on gloves and pulling out two steel batons about 24 inches long. The girls with the sexy haircuts took them, as the other two held down the barbers with the guns. One of the girls spoke in Spanish quietly. Then it was on! One slammed the end of the baton into Titus' stomach area sitting him up in agony and surprise; and then she dipped down to gain strength and gave Titus a crushing blow to his face and forehead area knocking him back in the chair and out cold. The other woman smiled and said something in Spanish as she swung the baton like a golf club into Titus. The other girl gave the one that mocked her, the finger with a smile, then a high five and laughed. One of the girls positioned Titus' head in the headrest, then each of them stood on the right and left side of his head about a foot back and began to pound his face and head area with synchronized brutality and force. Blood splattered up onto their faces, clothes, and on the mirror behind Titus' head, as the other barbers watched in complete horror. One of the barbers bent over and threw up right on the floor, as the girls holding them down with the guns smiled. After giving him about forty to fifty blows to the face and forehead area, they turned his dead body around and gave him about ten to fifteen blows to the top of his head before pulling out a gun and shooting him in what was left of his skull.

One of the girls with a gun looked at her watch and motioned for them to go. The bloody batons were placed in the gym bag. As the women walked toward the door, one of them walked up to one of the stunned barbers and told him in her Spanish accent to kiss her. When he refused from fear, she violently grabbed his face and gave him a wet nasty lick from his chin around to the side of his cheek.

"So sexy!" She said to him and walked toward the door following the other girls. Before she waked out she turned around and gave a matador-styled bow and exclaimed heartily, "Elvis has left the building!" and walked out.

~ · ~ · ~ · ~ · ~

Nate got the news later that same night and was ecstatic.

"Now that's how you run a fucking hit G: fly the killers in, bump the target, and fly the killers back out before the target gets a tag on his toe! That's how you do that shit!" Needless to say I wasn't impressed.

"Who were the killers?" I asked.

"Who the fuck cares? I talked to my man Hugo in Columbia, and we set it all up. I told him what I needed and he gave me a price that's all."

"I thought you wanted to be the one to do it?"

"Nah, I've gotten too big for that kind of shit G, plus you never know who would've snitched me out. Nah, don't need to take those kind of risks."

The next day the police found Titus and his dead bodyguards in the barbershop and made little effort to find the killers or investigate. Many people remembering the convenience store killings felt it was justice. They felt that Titus was a murdering gangbanger that got exactly what he deserved. The police were happy because it saved them a plethora of money and man hours looking for him and taxpayer money prosecuting him so everyone was happy – except…the Gangster Disciples. They were infuriated! On the street they figured Nate was responsible, and immediately upped the price on his head to one-hundred thousand dollars. But it didn't matter, by then Nate had unleashed his full fury on them through Dana and the South Side mafia.

The summer of 93' was the bloodiest summer in my recent memory. There were more black young men killed during that time than I care to remember. And these were not just murders; this was annihilation – a sort of crime-world cleansing – it really was …genocide. Dana and the South Side mafia committed heinous murders on the west side: men's heads were severed; women were gang raped in front of children; mothers, fathers and siblings that weren't even directly involved in crime were killed. Even babies, black babies were found in their cribs shot to death! From time to time different guys would try to tell me details from some of these murders and I would stop them; I just didn't want to hear it. All of it seemed demonic to me, like Dana and the mafia were possessed with some kind of evil or something. I knew guys would get clipped, but this was awful. Something inside of me got nauseated thinking about it. I would even have bad dreams of children, mothers crying out in horror from the things I knew that were going on. All of this to sell cocaine, it just wasn't worth it.

I prayed for the police to catch them before another innocent person or child died. But strangely the police were silent. There were news conferences, and comments from detectives, and a lot of lip service but nothing was actually done about it. I mean, can we really expect police in the city to really care about black folks killing black folks? Black on black crime has historically been met with lackluster response from law enforcement. I knew all of this, but it all seemed strange to me. How were we able to do all of this without so much as an arrest from anyone? I remember the investigation into Larry C's killing, but that was pushed more or less by detective Jackson and her group. There wasn't much support from the department. It all seemed very strange to me.

What was even stranger was the so-called crusade Dana took up while on the west side. It wasn't long, before Dana while on her killing spree made friends with some of the "working girls" over there. Some of the girls were hired to tip Dana off on the whereabouts of some the gangbangers and also told Dana how they were getting robbed by their so-called pimps. She was told of how they spent the whole night on their backs, and the pimps took all of the money, and got some of them hooked on drugs. So what does Dana do? She decides she would go and shake the pimps down and take their money and give it back to the hookers! She instituted a sort of street tax on the pimps so they could operate. The GD's by this time were so weak, that they had no choice but to be on the run for their own lives. Dana demanded sixty-five cents on the dollar for every pimp on the west side! Needless to say it's hard for a pimp to maintain their extravagant lifestyle on that kind of money, so a couple of them got cute and tried to kill Dana and botched it, which only made Dana really mad. The pimps that were responsible were hacked to death with axes. Other pimps that heard of this pretty much toed the line. I mean who the hell were they gonna run to? I witnessed one of these incidents first hand when I was sent to the west side by Nate under heavy security to see how things were going.

"What's up G? I'll talk to you in a minute," she said huffing and puffing on the stationary bike. The condo she rented was posh, with all of the luxuries, and toys. She liked to work out so, she had about fifty-thousand dollars worth of equipment in the joint. It was nice. Then there was a knock at the door. Some guy – obviously a pimp – came in, looking ragged, not as pompous as his kind usually looked. Dana got up from the bike and wiped her face, gave me the one minute signal and walked toward the bar where the pimp had stationed himself. Dana put one of her huge guns in the small of her back and sat down next to him at the bar as about five of her regime guys gathered around.

"Did you give Passion the money?" Dana asked slightly out of breath, sipping water.

"Uh, yeah, I gave her two-hundred. She only worked about two days, and she didn't make much. You know it's hard out there Dana. Guys ain't buying like they usually do, but I know she needs the money, so I helped her out, you know?"

"You know you're a lying piece of dog shit, pimp maggot motherfucker? My man talked to Passion earlier this morning and she told him you didn't give her anything; she was crying and said they turned her phone off this morning! She's over there with three kids with no phone, and you're gonna sit here and tell me you gave her two-hundred dollars and her fucking phone is off?"

"Uh, yeah Dana, I swear I gave her the money I...," The man started shaking.

"Don't lie to my Butch. I'll cut your fucking throat; you know I will. Don't fucking lie to me. Did you give her the money?" Dana was now agitated and loud. I couldn't believe what I was seeing! The man sheepishly nodded his head no. Angrily, Dana shouted, "You motherfucking-coward-pimp-piece-of-shit!" Two of the mafia guys hoisted the guy up and stuffed their hands in his pocket's and pulled out all he had and threw it on the bar. The money totaled about nine-hundred dollars. "Aw shit, this motherfucker holding out! Passion laying on her back making your sorry ass money and she don't get none?" Dana pistol whipped the guy and made him take all of his clothes off save his underwear and told him to leave.

"C'mon Dana don't do me like this. I ain't got no clothes on," the guy mumbled through obvious mouth wounds.

"Nigga, fuck you! You better get outta here while you can leave under your own power!" She fought back laughter drawing her gun to his face. As the guy stumbled toward the door, we all noticed shit stains in his underwear! Everyone burst into laughter; it was truly humiliating.

"Get your nasty, funky, black ass outta here bitch!" Dana said smiling putting her gun away as the whole room burst into laughter once again.

"What are you doing? You can't do the guy like that, he's gonna run to Nate. Nate knows that guy," I said to her.

"Oh yeah, I hope he washes his ass first," Dana said laughing.

"Dana you don't understand, Nate knows that guy. He ain't gonna like you doing him like that," I said.

Dana gave me a long look as her face changed from amusement to seriousness.

"You know it's good to see you bring your side line ass down to the front lines and tell me how to handle things G. You got problems with how I run shit down here? Go tell your brother!" she said.

"Dana you don't understand, that guys gonna run to Nate, and he didn't send you down here to shake down pimps, he sent you down here to...," I tried to explain again before she cut me off.

"I know what the fuck he sent me down here to do, man! I knew before you knew! Let me give you your report, so you can be up outta here. You're pissing me off!" She said loudly. Then one of the bodyguards that came with me handed me a cell phone. It was Nate on the other line; he frantically told me that Gabriella was in labor and that I should get home soon. I have to admit the disagreement I was having with Dana had been forgotten. I was really excited for Nate and I felt proud to be an uncle. I gave the guy the phone and I told Dana to stick the report and left.

Once I got back to New Lenox, I found Nate pacing in the kitchen biting his nails.

"G, what the fuck took you so long man. I thought you were gonna miss everything!" Nate said excitedly.

"That damn Dana, man. Do you know she's on the west side shaking down pimps?" I asked.

"What? Whatever. Look, Gabby's contractions are about a minute and a half apart, and the doctor and the nurses are up there and won't let me in. What the hell is all that about?" Nate asked.

"Well Nate you see…," I started to explain before I was interrupted by a crying newborn. Nate leaped straight up in the air like a wild man and ran up the stairs seemingly five steps at a time. Mike, Jon, and Pete came in running from downstairs and stopped at the staircase and gazed up.

"What did we have man"? Jon asked.

"I don't know. I better go up and see," I said. As I walked past the bodyguards into the room, I could see Nate had every amenity in the world in that room. It was set up exactly like a hospital room in case anything went wrong. Gabby was lying in the bed holding the baby while Nate kneeled beside her gazing at the newborn.

"It's a girl G, my own baby girl! Look, she looks like me and everything!" Nate said beaming with pride.

"You want to hold her baby?" Gabby said obviously exhausted.

"Oh boy, I don't know how…..come help me G," Nate said.

"*You* actually need help?" I said joking.

When Nate took that baby into his arms he started crying uncontrollably. He walked toward the window kissing her on the forehead to get a better look.

"Come here G, she's got eyes like mamma! Ain't she sweet man?" Nate said grinning and tearing.

"Yeah man. She looks like Mamma Williams, just like her," I said getting misty myself.

"See sweetie, that's your uncle G talking, say 'hi uncle G'," Nate said. It was the first time I had ever seen Nate in such a way. I could see for the first time that he had a tremendous amount of love in his heart hidden away,

that came out in a moment that seemed surreal. I threw my
arm around his shoulder and we both stood gazing at the
newborn like two mopes. "I wish mamma could see her G,
it breaks my heart that she didn't get to see her first
grandchild."

"When can we take her out doctor?" I asked.

"Well you better wait about two weeks or so, let
her get a little stronger. Then it should be ok," the doctor
explained.

Nate took the baby back to Gabby's waiting arms.
The baby was beautiful, I could see a combination of Nate,
Gabby, and Mamma Williams in her. It truly was a
wonderful feeling.

"God is truly awesome!" proclaimed Nate. I
looked at him strangely, it was the first time I had ever
heard him give any type of acknowledgement to God. But
this was a special moment for him, at this time Nate forgot
who he was and what he was. It was as if time stood still,
nothing else mattered, and I'll never forget it.

"Well Daddy, what are you gonna name her?"
Gabby asked looking at Nate. Nate stood looking at the
baby thinking for a minute.

"Gloria…Gloria Williams, after my mamma. What
do you think G?" he asked me.

"It's your child Nate, that's your call man," I
conceded. Actually I was a bit embarrassed that he asked
me what I thought and didn't ask Gabriella first.

"What do you think baby?" he said finally turning to
Gabby.

"I think it's a good name sweetie, but can we give
her a Spanish middle name?" Gabby asked sheepishly.

"Oh, yeah baby absolutely."

"I call her middle name Conchita, what do you think G?" Gabby asked me. Personally I didn't think it went well with Gloria, but who was I to say anything?

"Uh, it's cool Gabby. It sounds cool," I said lying.

"Gabby let's get married as soon as possible, after you get better ok?" Nate asked kneeling down next to her on the bed.

"Oh Nathan, yes I will marry you!" she said reaching out to him to kiss him through tears. "Right after I get back from California."

"California? What are you going there for?"

"Surgery baby. I gonna get a tummy tuck, and the lypo thing."

Nate looked at me strangely, and I shrugged my shoulders. Gabriella had always prided herself on her figure and she gained a significant amount of weight carrying the baby. As it turns out she had already spoke to a plastic surgeon there, and set it up for her to fly there about six months after having the baby. The thing that pissed Nate off was she didn't even discuss it with him. But even that couldn't get him mad on this day; he just shrugged it off.

After a couple of days, Mike and I went with Nate to Michigan Avenue to shop for some baby stuff and Gabby's wedding ring. I figured it would be a good time to fill him in on what was going on.

"You know Nate, Dana is really screwing up on the west side. She's over there shaking down pimps, and she and those mafia hoods are committing some grisly murders that I know you wouldn't ever sign off to. Do you know about any of this?" I asked.

"Uh, yes and no G. I gave Dana specific orders to do some things over there for us, but I gave her a little creative leeway you know…..think this will look good on the baby G?"

"Yeah…Nate…it's cute. But you know some of the shit is outrageous man. Everybody's talking about it, and these pimps, she's really fucking these guys up man. They found a pimp's head in the toilet in an apartment on Stony Avenue; did you know that?"

"Such are the hazards of our profession G……Gabby said I should get zero to three months; this outfit looks good but it's sized at six months, think I should get it?"

I could see he was totally preoccupied with his shopping, which kind of pissed me off. You see with Nate going gaga over the baby, I was left to handle things, and I know whenever he "snapped out of it" he was gonna expect everything to be handled properly. Which meant the pressure was all on me, and it pissed me off.

"Look Nate…," I said agitated.

"Be cool man, just let it go. He don't give a shit about nothing right about now. We'll just make sure shit doesn't get too out of hand, but he ain't hearing you right now," Mike whispered.

Little did Mike know shit was already out of hand. One of the Gangster Disciple lieutenants Nate had ordered Dana to murder was hiding out and had proven elusive for Dana. After about a month of unsuccessful attempts to find him, Dana kidnapped the guy's mother! Dana kept the old woman at her condo, and put the word on the street that she was held captive and would continue to be until the guy showed his face. Many people on the street felt Dana had crossed the line, and some of the other street gangs started to line up against us because of it. Needless to say on the way out of her condo one morning, a car drove by and unloaded about fourteen rounds Dana's way.

She escaped unscathed, but four of her guys were murdered, as well as innocent passersby. Once again the fallout was tremendous.

Many of the county and city officials were alerted about the violence that plagued the city streets, and the number of murders within the recent months. It was announced that they were gonna crack down on gang violence immediately. After the attempt on her life, Dana had given an order to murder the old lady she had been holding captive, but I stopped her.

"Fuck you, G. I don't take no orders from you; get me Nate on the phone!" she said.

"Look, Nate has me in charge, and he gives me full power over both regimes and their capo's. That includes you! Now don't touch that old lady, as a matter of fact tomorrow morning let her go. She has nothing to do with this war," I shouted back.

"Well you can kiss my ass G, I ain't budging!" She said before hanging up the phone. Well after she pulled that shit, I sent Mike up there to bring the guys from her regime back and told Jon to pull the plug on the finances. The next thing you know Dana is in New Lenox demanding to speak to Nate. Nate, Dana, and I go into the office and we all have it out once and for all.

"First of all, this war is costing us in areas we can't afford. Pete said sales are suffering, and it's hard to keep people high and happy if they fear for their lives. The fucking heat she is bringing down is unbelievable. We had police who were cooperative and informants helping out. Now everyone fears for their lives and it makes it hard to make a buck Nate," I reasoned.

"That's bullshit! Nate what's right is right. These motherfuckers tried to hit me last week, so I hit them back. I had the old lady holed up in the condo trying to draw this gang motherfucker out and it was working nice until G's ass pulled my men! You sent me to the west side to take control. This motherfucker wants to play paddy cake with these niggers and it won't work! Now Nate, you gave me all that I needed to wage this war and we were winning now he has set me back!" Dana said angrily.

"What do you propose Dana? G is in charge," Nate said calmly holding the baby.

"I want my men, and my money back and I want that old woman and her gangbanging-ass son dead!" Dana shouted.

"Lower your voice Dana, you'll scare the baby," Nate said sternly. Then Gabriella came in and gave Nate and I a stern look and took the baby from him. She told him that she wanted to see him when we were finished. We could tell she was angry. Nate put his head into his hand for a moment and then addressed us. "First, the lieutenant is dead; Mike and his guys hit him about four this morning in Markham. Second, the old lady has to die G, she will finger Dana especially after she finds out her son is dead. And you know my motto: 'it's always better with no witnesses.'" Nate grabbed a beer from the bar.

"Nate I hear that lady is sixty-eight, she is no threat to us," I reasoned.

"I don't give a damn if she is one-hundred and eight. She can see, can't she? That's the whole point G. She'll finger Dana and some of the mafia guys. She's gotta go!"

I shook my head in disgust. Nate could see my frustration and dismissed Dana.

"Dana I promise you will be back online by tomorrow night. Go back up there and we'll try to wrap this shit up ok?"

"Cool, no more interruptions, right?" Dana asked.

"I gave you my word Dana," Nate replied. With that she walked out of the office. I just sat on the sofa in despair and defeat. "G, it's gonna be ok. You'll see. We're about a week from ending the west side thing and we will have peace again."

"Until when? How long will we have peace Nate? We are in the drug business; there is no peace in this business remember?" I said as I walked out of the room.

~ · ~ · ~ · ~ · ~

The next few weeks Dana with the go-ahead from Nate, murdered about fifteen to twenty more gang chieftains. The local police cracked down on gang violence within the city by rounding up the small number of gangbangers that Dana hadn't killed. Many Gangster Disciples were indicted on a litany of counts: murder, racketeering, conspiracy, and a lot more. But not so much as a parking ticket for any of our people. And that is what was so strange to me; even gang members from groups that we were allies with were being harassed and arrested. I mean they never talked, but the irony of it was too strange. Nate was so into his new daughter that he really didn't know what was going on, I handled all of the day to day business. *And* there was a lot of it. Crack cocaine was making us a fortune, but because of his baby, Nate never enjoyed any of it. When the baby was a bit older Nate and I took her to the cemetery to Mamma Williams' gravesite. Standing at the gravesite I thought it would be a good time to ask Nate about a few things, and let him know how business was going.

"You know we are closing in on about sixty million Nate. I talked to Jon and he suggested opening some businesses in other counties to wash a little more money."

"Maybe that would be a good idea, although it's pretty tough to hide sixty million dollars. Jon is doing a great job," Nate replied looking down at Mamma Williams' headstone.

"You know G, we should get our moms bigger headstones. I really wish mamma could see the baby. I know she would love her. I really miss her a lot," he said despondently.

"Yeah, so do I. Things have changed so much in the last few years Nate, thinking about it makes my head spin."

Nate handed off the baby to me and kneeled down. He began cleaning off the headstone and gravesite with some gardening tools we brought with us. It was a tranquil day, and there was no one around except the mafia bodyguards. It felt good to just share with Nate without Dana, Mike and the others around to interfere and distract, so I felt it was as good a time as any to address Nate with my chief concerns.

"Nate, can we talk about something?" I asked.

"Sure G, whats on your mind?"

"Well….how are we able to do all of this? I mean don't you think we have been unusually lucky that none of us have gone down? Especially since the GD's, and some of our friends in the business are catching hell?"

"Well G, I think it's great. Do you really want any of us to go to jail? This hasn't exactly been a cakewalk you know."

"True, but don't you think it has been strangely easy? We're pushing all of this crack on the community, with not so much as a parking ticket." I reasoned.

"What do you call my arrest a couple of months ago G?" Nate said stopping to look up at me.

"Yeah I know, but that had nothing to do with our drug sales, much less all of these murders since. It's almost as if we had some help from somewhere."

"That's ridiculous G, we are doing this because we are doing it right. We are not taking unnecessary risks like the gangbangers and...," Nate tried to finish his banter before I cut him off.

"I'm not buying it Nate; I know our capabilities. I know what criminals are able to do. We are pushing hundreds of pounds of cocaine on the community under the thunderous sound of silence. No write-ups in the papers, no indictments, no press, no stakeouts, no reporters, it just doesn't make sense."

"G, you worry too much." Nate continued to clean the headstone.

I didn't say anything. Although it annoyed me that whenever I asked serious questions everyone told me that I worried too much, I found it dismissive. After cleaning the headstone, Nate went on to talk to his mother about baby and her birth. I picked up the garden tools and walked toward my mother's headstone and began to clean it. All of a sudden I was engulfed with emotion and began to cry.

"I'm sorry momma, I am so sorry. I know you didn't want me to turn out like this; I know you didn't want this for me. I miss you so much, I wish you could find a way out of this life for me. If you are in heaven, can you give me a sign or something? I feel so rotten and dirty. I feel like I am damned, and there is no way out. I feel trapped. Mamma, if there is any way to redeem myself, show me. I promise I will walk away from this life forever!" I sobbed. I felt lost. I felt I had committed the most heinous crime of all; I was no longer true to myself.

Nothing in the world matters in life if you don't feel good about who you are. If you hate yourself and the way you live, all the money in the world doesn't matter. I knew my mother would've been ashamed of me for turning out this way. Sure she was hooked on drugs, but she turned to drugs out of hopelessness, despair, and fear. I felt I did a terrible disservice to my mother because I saw what drugs did to her, I saw what it did to our lives. Now I was helping to do it to thousands of other women just like my mother. Once when I was a kid I swore if I ever saw the guy that sold my mother drugs, I would kill him when I became a man. What did I do, I became the very scum that helped to destroy my mother. Kneeling down at my mother's gravesite, I came full circle with myself. I had been slapped into the reality of what I really had become, a murderous drug dealing animal, but I didn't know how to stop. I didn't know what steps to take, what to say, what to do.

"Let's go G, you ready?" Nate said tapping me on the shoulder, giving me a piece of tissue.

"How long you been standing there?" I asked sniffing.

"I just walked up. You ready, it's getting dark, I think it's gonna rain or something."

"Yeah, I'm ready. Bye mamma, I'll talk to you later," I whimpered.

As we walked to the limo I noticed that the mafia guy carrying the baby with the car seat glanced at me strangely, and threw his head back down. At the time I didn't think too much of it, I had tons of other things on my mind. In the car Nate lightened the mood by starting to talk about the White Sox.

"You know my boys are looking a little better this year, they might even make the playoffs, huh?" Nate asked looking at me.

"Yeah maybe," I said looking out of the window. He didn't say anything else, I guess he could tell I wasn't much for talking.

Back at the house Dana met us at the front entrance to the estate gleaming and grinning, with Mike and Gabby. As we got out of the car Gabby took the baby from the mafia guy and started toward the inside.

"Gabby I want to talk to you," Nate said before she went in.

"I'll be upstairs."

Dana walked up to Nate and whispered something in his ear. Nate pursed his lips and gave her a nod of approval as we all walked in. I found out later that Dana was telling that the family was officially in control of the west side. Most of the Gangster Disciples' leaders had been killed or prosecuted by authorities, which left the gang significantly weakened. The GD's were given a block here and there to sell, but the family controlled the rest. We had a meeting later that night to discuss the news. It was then that I learned the family's next move.

"Ok, Dana has told me that we are officially controlling shit on the west side now. All of our detractors, enemies, and critics have been silenced thanks in part to the Chicago police, and the state boys. We are now free to make our profits, and become the organization we set out to be," Nate announced. Everyone stood and clapped. As I stood I just looked around at everyone else. "We owe our gratitude to Dana and her regime for a job well done; she took complete control of the west side single-handedly, and did it without losing too many men, so let's give her a hand," Nate said smiling. Dana and a couple of her chieftains held up their drinks acknowledging the applause. "However there is one more fish we have to fry…that fucking-cop-bitch-detective Jackson. It's time for us to cancel her fucking contract," Nate said angrily.

"Yeah it's time for that bitch to go to sleep," Pete said in agreement.

"Jon has been talking to some of our friends and they have agreed to help finance the killing so that won't be a problem. We just need a good plan," Nate said.

"I got a few of my boys watching her and recording her habits and shit. If you all give me a month or so I will have her routine down," Mike asserted.

"Good, that will help tremendously in coming up with a plan," Nate said.

Personally I didn't think it was a good idea. We had defeated everyone and had most of Chicago locked down, is it really necessary to gun down a Chicago police detective? However, Nate made up his mind and seemed to have the rest of the crew on his side so I said nothing. I don't think it would have made a difference anyway, what I thought really never did.

The next week or so was spent planning the killing. Many guys in the criminal world wanted Jackson dead, because of the heat she had bought down on them over the years. Much of her harassment rarely resulted in convictions, but all the same, many dealers felt she had to go. I talked to some of our people to see what they felt about the move. Everyone was for it except for Jon surprisingly. He felt that it was one tree we need not climb.

"I'm just not for it G. She's a cop and that might prove to be our undoing," Jon warned.

"I feel the same way. I mean she isn't taken very seriously down at the department and things are quieting down on the street. I don't know why we need to do this," I lamented.

Jon felt if it had to be done let someone else do it and take the risk.  Since I had an ally in this, I decided maybe Jon and I should take it to Nate and maybe we might be able to persuade him to change his mind.

"No, fuck No!  That bitch has to go, and it ain't negotiable," Nate said emphatically.

"Nate I know how you feel, but she's a cop man. We might be buying the farm on this one," Jon warned. During our discussion, Gabby came in with the baby and sat on the sofa in the office.

"Hey give us a minute baby, I'll be up in a minute," Nate said.

"Ok, but you have to go to bed, and you haven't taken your medicine," Gabby said motherly.

"Medicine?  What's wrong man?" I asked.

"Nothing man, I think I am coming down with the flu or something."

"Oh.  Well, at least think about what we are saying, Nate.  Just consider it." Jon petitioned.

"Yeah, whatever."  Nate grumbled as he rose to walk out of the office.

I didn't linger around.  I had a date with a chick I met at one of our clubs.  We decided to take in a movie and have dinner at the Cheesecake Factory downtown.  Mike assigned three bodyguards to me and I went out on my date.  Everything went fine until I got to the restaurant. After a couple of cognacs and some conversation with my date, none other than Detective Jackson walks toward me clearly under the influence and rudely sits down right at my table!  She looked wired, like she hadn't had any sleep in a couple of days, and her breath smelled.

"Well, fancy meeting you here, small world isn't it?"  She slurred.

"What the fuck do you want? Don't you see I am on a date?" I snapped.

"I just want to ask a question. How did you do it?"

"Do what, what are you talking about?" I asked agitated.

"How did you get the doctor to change his story, what did you say to him?"

"You know detective, I have witnesses here that will attest to you harassing me. I suggest you leave before I call my lawyer," I warned.

"Fuck your lawyer. I want to know how you did it? Well, it doesn't matter, I am coming back after you and your brother, but this time you won't escape. And if you do, I'll try again, and again, and again until I nail both of you...if it takes my whole career."

At that moment, I looked into her eyes and through the alcohol and could see she wasn't kidding. She was actually going to devote her life to collaring us.

"You have a nice evening, drug dealer!" She slurred as she got up to walk away.

Needless to say I was very embarrassed, which I understood was part of her objective. Although I really didn't care for Jackson, I pitied her. We had helped to destroy her career and her son's reputation just so we could sell drugs. I knew she was right. We are drug dealers and we all belonged in jail. I was never one to delude myself into rationalizing crimes like most people in this business do. I knew that soon our luck would run out and she would finally get us behind bars, especially since no other law enforcement people seemed to care what we did in this city. But I couldn't have that because if Nate went to jail, he wouldn't last a week; they would kill him before me. And like it or not Nate was all the family I had left on this earth. He was my brother and I still held out hope that we would get out of this life one day. I couldn't let Jackson destroy that, I just couldn't. It was right there that I too understood that she had to go.

When I got back to the house I told Jon about my encounter with Jackson.

"Well whatever, I still think we should let her go," Jon said.

"Jon I agree but we can't, this bitch is sick. Look what we did to her: her career and her son's reputation are ruined. She's out for revenge you know – vendetta."

"Yeah, yeah I know all of that G, but she's still a cop. They would have our asses. All of the cops on payroll, our informants, everyone would run for cover. I don't know if we can risk it." Jon said as he smoked his joint.

"I can't let my brother go to jail, I just can't."

"Then come up with a plan," Mike said as he entered the room. As I turned around I could see Mike and Dana walking in with Harold's chicken again.

"Where is Nate, is he coming down?" Dana asked.

"Nah, Gabby said he is sick…matter of fact he won't be involved in this one at all. He wants you to come up with the plan and carry it out G," Mike announced.

"Me…why me?" I asked surprised.

"He thinks you would be the most technical; you would make sure it is done right; and that no one would be carried off. But you got one month that's all," Mike said.

"Fuck this, I need to talk to him, I ain't having this shit," I said angrily.

"Fine, but Gabby ain't gonna let you talk to him, and you definitely ain't getting past those dogs. What's up man? Just do the shit G. It ain't no big deal," Mike said.

"Yeah, let's just buck this bitch and get it over with!" Dana said chewing. I picked up my drink and excused myself and started toward the staircase to go up to my room.

"Fine, Mike I need that intelligence report from you and your people tomorrow morning," I said as I walked up the stairs. As much as I didn't want to, I had to, or so I thought at the time. Jackson wasn't letting up on us, and I just couldn't risk Nate nor myself going to jail. She had been transferred to another area, but once we did what we did to her and her son I knew she wasn't going to stop until she had us.

I had heard Nate plan for killings before, even witnessed Dana and Nate kill some guys, but had never planned a murder myself. Killing Jackson wasn't going to be like killing a gangbanger or a fellow guy in the "business". This had to be different. She was a police detective, a highly visible detective. It had to be carefully planned and thought out, and some money was going to have to be spent. I didn't want to fly in people for this because I didn't have the connections Nate had. I was going to have to use our people, which posed a problem. Dana was far too crude, and Mike didn't have the stomach for it, unless she did something to him. So I set my plan and got a "budget" for the killings like Nate had taught us to do from Jon. I figured I could pull it off for forty grand. Jon approved it without any problems and I went to work.

I figured the South Side mafia was some of the most feared killers in Chicago, and highly trained. Why not use them? I decided to get about six guys from Dana's regime to train and prepare them for the killing. One of the things I learned from history was whenever an official had to be murdered, no one could be caught; no one could ever be indicted, or bought up on any charges. The killers had to walk away free, then they had to be sacrificed and murdered as well.

I had heard of gang boys killing cops before, but they always got caught, that's not how we did things in the family. I figured the mafia members were pretty much expendable; I would spend about a month training them for the hit, make Mike and Dana supervise it and kill those involved. But before I could do that I had to mentally detach myself from the whole situation. I couldn't think about it too much or I wouldn't be able to do it.

The intelligence Mike gave me on Jackson was superb; his people gave me a day-by-day itinerary of her whereabouts. I figured the best day to do it would be Saturday – that was her day to go work out. She always went to the club in Hyde Park, so we figured we could get her on 47$^{th}$ Street. The closest police station in the area was on 51$^{st}$ so we would have a little time. But we had to be careful to make sure no cops were around. I got six guys from the mafia to train in riding speed motorcycles. I had them riding next to cars at forty to fifty miles an hour while firing paint ball shots into them. A couple of the guys fell off and injured themselves but soon they had it down. The escape had to be as clean as the killing, so I had Mike and Dana on the scene to make sure things went ok. After about a month and a half we had everything ready. We practiced it over and over until I was satisfied with the results.

On a sunny Saturday morning, May 15$^{th}$ 1994, Detective Jackson met her fate.

## CHAPTER 5

## KING NATHAN

Early that morning I was nervous. *What if things didn't go right? What if someone was caught? What if we missed the target?* I had to put all of that out of my mind though; I had a job to do, and the biggest question of all I kept asking myself was....*what if we tried to kill her and she lived?* I ate a light breakfast and sent Dana, Mike, and the six mafia guys into Chicago to get into their places.

**6am**

Mike's job was to position himself on the rooftop across the street with binoculars to let the cyclists know when the mark was coming down 47$^{th}$ Street. According to intelligence the mark usually made her turn onto 47$^{th}$ near King Drive and would then head eastbound to the gym. Dana's job was to position herself on the ground and coordinate the cyclists through their route, supervise and witness the killing, and make sure the cyclists got on the route back to the compound. Jackson was a very well known detective in the community – not well liked, however well known. We knew that police in the area would rush to her aid if she radioed them in despair, so we had an operative sabotage her car radio late the previous night. Also, we had another operative to send in a bomb threat to Area One headquarters and set off a couple of M80 bombs in some garbage cans for a distraction just before our attack. Nothing was left to chance. It was planned beautifully. Almost all of the cops were pulled off the street and moved toward Area One headquarters on 51$^{st}$ Street. The hit men and Dana stopped at a safe house we had on 69$^{th}$ Street to get dressed and prepare. A moving truck carried the hit men and their cycles to 47$^{th}$ Street. Another member of Dana's regime stood on the corner near the area of the shooting to let Mike know on the rooftop if everything was ok. His job was important because he had the view of everything; the street, all passersby, any cops coming through, and he would have the birds eye view of the killing. If all systems were go, an operative on the street was to open a newspaper, then Mike would radio all of the cyclists and Dana by saying "Green, Green, Green"; and if the man on the street tucked his newspaper under his arm that would signal Mike to tell all of those involved to "Abort, Abort, Abort". We had practiced this day and night for a month; we were ready. All pieces were in place, all we needed now was the mark.

**7:30am**

Detective Jackson was spotted at an intersection near King Drive just as expected. As she made her turn onto 47$^{th}$ Street we were immediately alerted. As I listened in on the radio and communication we had set up, I began to get extremely nervous and felt something might go wrong. As I listened intensely, Nate walked slowly into the room with a huge robe on and a cup of tea and a towel wrapped around his neck. I felt his hand rest on my shoulder as I leaned in to get a better reception through the static.

"Is everything good?" He asked through a raspy and obviously sore throat.

"Yeah...Yeah," I quickly shot back and waved him off. I didn't want to get distracted from the next five to seven minutes because they were crucial.

**7:34am**

As the mark approached Vernon Avenue, it was spotted that someone else was in the car.

"G we got a passenger," one of the operatives said through the radio.

"Give me details, quickly," I said anxiously.

"Looks like a guy, maybe the same age as the mark…wait she just gave him a kiss. I'm guessing he is a boyfriend, what you want done?" The operative stated through minimal static. I quickly looked up at Nate and he quickly raked his index finger across his throat signaling that he wanted the companion killed. I told the operative the order and he immediately told all involved that there were now two marks, but the passenger; the boyfriend had to be killed first. This was imperative because if we shot the driver first, the passenger might reach for a cell phone and call the authorities, but if the passenger was killed first, Jackson would probably reach for her radio which had been disabled long before she would reach for a cell phone. It would buy us time. Now the marks were approaching the kill zone. Dana and the other cyclists zoomed out of the back of the moving truck and onto 47<sup>th</sup> Street just in front of the mark. The cycles they were riding were black and red speed bikes, and Dana and the other killers were dressed in red leather jumpsuits and dark-tinted helmets so they couldn't be identified. The cyclists along with Dana were stopped at a light just before the kill zone, they allowed the mark to ride slightly ahead of them so they could speed up and gain complete access. There was supposed to be a killer riding next to the passenger side, and one behind the car. Both were to fire into the car at the same time, to create a sort of crossfire giving the mark little chance to recover and give any return fire. They were instructed to ride at least a three-to-five-foot distance from the vehicle, and they were given handgun styled double barrel shotguns with pistol grips for maximum power. The mark could not be allowed to live or escape.

## 7:36am...The Kill

As the marks approached the kill zone, my heart started thumping, and my hands were sweaty. Nate seemed quite relaxed as he sipped his tea, listening to the action, lightly tapping his foot on the floor.

"Thirty seconds to shot," Mike said calmly over the radio. I closed my eyes and started to sweat from my brow. Part of me hoped something would go wrong, but it couldn't if she survived a murder attempt she would surely believe it was us, she had to die. "Target," Mike said sternly which meant for the passenger side cyclist to move into position. And then five seconds of silence. Then......"Green! Green! Green!" Mike said in quick forceful succession. The passenger side cyclist whipped out his shotgun and fired two powerful shots that sounded like cannons over the radio. I could hear people screaming on the streets and yelling as the first shot shattered the glass, and then lodged into the boyfriend's neck. The second shot practically ripped his head off of his body. Jackson screamed in frantic despair as she tried to control the car, radio for help and assist her dying friend. Blood had spattered all over the front window and the side windows but left the back clear for the rear cyclist's view. The rear cyclist whipped out his shotgun and aimed for Jackson's head and fired, the first shot thrusted her forward as it hit her in the upper back and shoulder area. The rear cyclist quickly fired another shot that tore open the left side of Jackson's head. Needless to say, the car was out of control and slammed into an idle city garbage truck as

Jackson's body came almost completely out of the front window. There was pandemonium on the streets as people screamed and took cover in a state of horror. The complete kill took only two and a half minutes. Dana gave the thumbs up to Mike and his crew on the roof. The operative on the street folded his paper and quickly walked toward an ominous unmarked car and drove off. Mike and his rooftop crew quickly disassembled all camera and radio equipment and headed downstairs in a frenzy and hopped into an equally ominous SUV and drove off. The cyclists and Dana speed off and onto Lake Shore Drive on the 47$^{th}$ Street entrance as planned. They all got away and everything went according to plan.

"Good job G, real good job," Nate said in his hoarse, sickly voice as he patted me on the shoulder and walked off to get back into bed. I slumped back into the chair and rubbed the sweat from my brow, and exhaled. It was all over. All of Nate's enemies had been "handled" and he had complete control of the south and west sides of Chicago.

All of the criminal culture in Chicago bended to his power and authority, as insiders now began to refer to him as "King Nathan." He was the gold standard in terms of drug distributors in the Midwest.

We spent the next two days killing all of the operatives and cyclists that were involved in the murder. Their bodies were dumped and left for the police to find. In one of the guy's pockets Dana put in a map of 47$^{th}$ Street and circled the area of the murder and wrote "Kill Zone" in red. The police were confident that they had the killers, but lamented that they didn't have a motive. Many on the force knew there had to be someone larger behind the killing, but they had no clue as to who it was. Nate eventually recovered from his flu episode and took a trip to

California with Gabby and the baby. Our drug profits were pouring in and everyone couldn't have been happier.

Nate officially proposed to Gabby and had a private ceremony at the compound and only Nate's friends in the "Business" were invited. Gabby had phoned her mother in Columbia and told her about her getting married and the new baby. She told me how her mother was ecstatic to hear form her and the news about the baby, but remained indifferent about her lifestyle. Nate pulled out all of the stops for the wedding and reception. There were decorations everywhere; he even made Gabby take stepping lessons for the big day. He asked me to find a preacher to come to the house to perform the ceremony, and when I suggested Rev. Fisher he exploded.

"Fuck no! You know I can't stand his ass G, why would you even bring him up?" He said scathing.

"Well, he's the only one I know," I retorted.

"What about some of the ones we work with?" he asked.

"Shit man I thought you wanted a real preacher for something this important. I didn't think you wanted to fuck with no jackleg bootleg preachers."

"I don't care, all he has to do is come in and mouth the words and perform the ceremony. Whether he is real or not is up to him and God," Nate reasoned.

"But Nate if he ain't real, your vows aren't real. They both go hand-in-hand." But he didn't listen; he ended up getting some bootleg from the city to officiate the vows. Gabby wore a beautiful gown, and the rest of us were dressed up and looking dignified. Even Dana put on a dress and heals. She looked about as comfortable and graceful as an oxen, but she managed to pull it off. At the reception we all partied heavy.

Nate had one of the house nannies put little Gloria to sleep in another part of the house. Mike and Dana went to go check on her every few minutes or so to make sure she was ok. We all loved little "Glo" as we all affectionately called her. She was truly adorable. She was closing in on one year now and had shed the newborn look, and was a full-fledged toddler now. Nate loved her immensely; he would spend hours with her. Tickling, playing, drawing, whatever it took, he was there. I could sense that he was starting to change, at least on the surface. Maybe the killing and posturing and trouble that he had been into for the last few years was starting to wear him down? But it didn't matter; we were all in too deep now. There was no other way out for us but death, so I thought.

**Cook County Morgue shortly after the killing:**

"Ok, pull that sheet back," Inspector Trent demanded. As the aid pulled the sheet back, Trent recoiled in shock. The complete left side of Detective Jackson's head had been blasted out and her eyes were still open with a look of terror transfixed on her lifeless body. "Ok, that's enough. I've seen enough," Trent resigned.

"Harry what the hell happened out there today?" Jackson's former partner asked fighting back tears.

"I wish like hell I knew. I tell you the fucking violence in this city has reached a fever pitch. I knew Diane had enemies, but I would have never thought something like this would happen."

"The press is down the hall waiting for you. The chief of police and the mayor have already made their statements. What will you say?"

"I don't know."

At that time, the police appeared with Detective Jackson's son for him to identify the body of his mother.

"Does he have to do this now?" Trent said angrily.

"Well yes sir.  He wanted to, actually," the officer said hesitantly.  Trent looked at the young man with deep empathy, then beckoned him and placed his hands squarely on the young man's shoulders and proceeded to talk to him in a fatherly tone.

"You don't have to do this you know.  Your mom's sister and other relatives are on their way down here.  I really don't think it is a good idea for you to do this, son."

"I....I want to.  I want to see what they did to her," the young man said choking back tears.  He walked away from Trent and walked toward the table, took a deep breath and motioned for the aid to pull back the sheet.  After looking at her, he began to sob aloud and started to mumble her name softly.  He was obviously traumatized as Trent moved quickly to gently remove him from the room.  As they left the room, members of the press spotted them and started toward them.

"I have no comments right now; I will address you later," Trent said waving his hand and guiding the boy down the cold and dreary hall.

Obviously the killing dominated the evening news that night.  Politicians made statements and policemen expressed outrage and vowed revenge.  The mayor insisted that the killers would be hunted down and justice would be swift and exact.  As we watched the evening news that night, Nate smoked a cigar and expressed no emotion at all, as if he had nothing to do with the killing.  Dana smirked and said that Jackson had received just what was coming to her.  Mike agreed especially since Jackson had botched the investigation into Donnell's murder years ago.  Gabby sat and rocked baby Glo as she shook her head introspectively.

"So much violence," she said softly. Gabby knew what we were into, but Nate had given strict instructions not to let her know any specifics. Consequently she had no knowledge of the family's involvement. Jon and Pete sat motionless as members of the mafia stared into the wide screen television like mannequins. For the first time I believe it was sinking in what we were and how low we had sunk. Jackson's son approached the throng of reporters outside of police headquarters with Trent next to him and gave a statement.

"My mother served this city all of her life. All she wanted was to be a cop. She made mistakes but her loyalty to this city and its citizens was never in question. Although I hate what they did to her, I forgive the people who did this. I only hope God will have mercy on their souls. I have nothing more." As he walked away, Trent approached the throng. Nate leaned in slowly twirling the cigar gently in his mouth trying to hear what Trent had to say.

"Detective Jackson was a tough cop that we will miss greatly, but as the mayor has said we will find the people responsible for this act and exact justice. The people of Chicago can rest assure of this." He never looked into the cameras.

"Humph, fucking coward," Nate said smugly. The general consensus on the street was one of numbness from the common folk; people were right – Jackson had enemies, but many felt her murder was too heinous and barbaric to show any signs of happiness or resolve. Even for us, we were all kind of quiet. "Turn that shit off," Nate said rising up from the couch and breaking the silence. Nate went to get his dogs for a walk; I decided I would go with him. I could sense he wanted to talk.

As we strolled down the designated area for the dogs, Nate said nothing. He just puffed away at his cigar. So, I decided I would speak first.

"You ok?"

"Yeah, I'm cool. I just needed a little air that's all." Nate looked around for the bodyguards. We walked and really didn't say anything for about five minutes or so, just taking in the air and looking at those beastly dogs of his.

"You know G, I thought bucking that bitch would have made me feel better, but it really didn't. I mean looking at all of that coverage tonight on the news, it felt.....weird."

"What do you mean?"

"It all just made me think, you know? It made me think about a lot of shit."

"Like what?"

"Well, it made me think about mamma for one. You know if someone had killed my mom like that I would have grabbed my gat and went after the first motherfucker I could find, but this dude...I don't know," Nate said referring to Jackson's son and shaking his head.

"Then I thought about Gabby and little Glo. What if someone had tried to hurt them? You know having a family makes you think about a lot of shit. Before, I could do this shit and eat a steak dinner and go up in a couple of broads and sleep like a baby. But now there's Gabby, and the baby and shit......I just don't know," Nate said confused. For the first time, Nate was starting to consider the consequences of our actions. I wasn't gonna let him off that easily, so like he had done with me so many times before I gave reason for the madness.

"Nate the family is worth about sixty million dollars collectively," I said.

"And...*shit* we can't go anywhere to spend it! G we are prisoners in that big ass house, I can't take Gabby and the baby anywhere without worrying about getting shot or worse something happening to them. Sometimes the ends don't seem to justify the means." Well, he wasn't gonna get any sympathy from me, I had been trying to tell him this for years. If having a family was now beginning to help him understand what the hell was going on so be it. I just looked down and kicked a couple of rocks and listened as he went on. "And that fucking hit, you know maybe we should have let one of the gangs handle that shit," Nate said disgusted.

"You know they would have fucked it up Nate; we had to do it. She was coming after us again and this time maybe she would have succeeded."

"Yeah, maybe." Nate put what was left of his cigar out with his foot.

"Well if it's any consolation you're the man now, the head nigger in charge. You're on top of the world baby!" I said smiling.

"Yeah, I am. Ain't I? Well, to the victor go the spoils! Let's head back. Let's eat, drink, and be merry for tomorrow we die!" Nate said lightening the mood and smiling. Truer words had never been spoken.

## Jackson's Funeral

The turnout for Jackson's funeral was surprising. Hundreds of people gathered on the streets while cops decked in their dress blues marched and the bagpipes played. The mood was expectedly sorrowful as it began to drizzle lightly. Everyone in the Hyde Park community seemed shaken. They all knew Jackson, and many disapproved of her actions at times, but they knew if they were ever in a jam Jackson would help them out. She was one of those cops you didn't particularly care for, but knew you could count on. There were wreaths and bouquets of flowers lying near the area where the shooting took place. There were reporters, civic activists, and politicians everywhere. I believe even Jackson would have been surprised by the turnout. After Diane Jackson's body was laid to rest, Trent was handed a cell phone by a fellow officer.

"This is for you," the unknown officer said. Trent looked at him strangely, trying to place his face, and understand why a complete stranger would hand him a cell phone. The voice on the other end was that of an older gentleman with a Bostonian Harvard accent.

"Harry, is this you?" the gentleman asked.

"Yes?" Trent answered meekly.

"Good. Meet me at Cob Hill tomorrow. We will be teeing off at about noon. You be there by eleven-thirty," the older man said before abruptly ending the call.

## Cob Hill 11:25am

"How are you, Harry?"

"Good sir and yourself?" Trent asked sheepishly.

"Fair to midland, you know I visited my doctor yesterday. I've been cancer free for ten years now."

"That's great sir; it's good to hear that considering the news I have been handed down," Trent said sadly.

"Yeah I heard about that. Well if I can beat it you surely can." The man feigned concern. The older man scanned Trent up and down as he tossed golf clubs into a beautiful leather golf bag. "What the fuck happened out there Harry?"

"We don't know precisely sir….we're still trying to iron things out." Trent barely made eye contact looking at all of the bodyguards around with earpieces.

"My ass! You know what the fuck happened out there and who the fuck was behind it! Diane was an asshole true, but she was still blue! And that shit can never happen to blue Harry!" The man gritted teeth as he looked around to see if anyone was listening. Clearly intimidated, Trent picked up a couple of golf clubs and gently placed them in the older man's golf bag. "Harry, I think it's time we begin to end our little experiment, don't you think?" Trent sheepishly nodded his head in agreement, never looking the older man in the eye.

"Can I ask a favor sir?" Trent said looking at the man for the first time.

"What is it?" the man said impatiently.

"Is there anyway we can spare the boys? I promised their mother years ago I would...," Trent said before he was interrupted.

"That nigger hooker that died of AIDS on the south side years ago? Harry I can't promise that. I won't promise that and you know it."

"Please sir, you know I wouldn't ask this of you if it wasn't important," Trent pleaded.

"You know it sickens me to see you more loyal to two nigger bastards than you are to your own wife and kids! Get out of my sight!" The older man said dismissively. Just then another gentleman walked up to the older man and slapped him on the back surprising him.

"How many eagles today, Logan?" The clean cut dapper man asked the older gentleman with a boyish charm.

"Who knows, maybe eighteen!" The older gentleman smiled and then nodded Trent to leave the area. As Trent left the area and walked along the warm golf course his life flashed before him. He was emotionally beaten and broken. Wiping his brow he thought about the last twenty years and what he had accomplished and in an instant he summed it all up....to nothing. He glanced at the suited bodyguards as they watched him carefully walk toward his car. He looked up at the beaming sun and at Jackson's former partner sitting on the passenger side of his late model vehicle.

"What was all of that about?" the young man asked as Trent sat in the car.

"Life...it was about life," Trent sighed.

"Huh, what do you mean?" The young man beleaguered.

"You know, I learned more about life up on that hill five minutes ago than I have learned in a lifetime."

"Hmmm, who was that guy? He looks real important."

"If I told you, I'd have to kill you," Trent said with a sly grin as he started the car and drove off.

## CHAPTER 6

## ...AND MERCURY FALLS

The spring of '96 was great. The Chicago Bulls and Michael Jordan were about to win their sixth championship in eight years and the city of Chicago couldn't be happier – although the grip of drugs had paralyzed the city, particularly the black community. What hurt the most was we were responsible for about eighty-five to ninety percent of those drugs hitting the streets. Never before had we seen so many "Hypes" and "zombies" fill the streets begging for quarters, nickels, anything to feed their habit. Many even used their kids to get money. Mike and Dana would come back with stories of women selling their daughters to our drug dealers as payment for a hit of the pipe. Women were becoming hookers and men were giving oral sex to other men for some "rock". The stories were horrific, but necessary because it had been better than seven years since Nate had been to Chicago or the old 'hood. He didn't know or see firsthand what we were doing to our own people.

Seventy-first Street near Park Manor, where we grew up, was only a shell of what it once was. When we were kids the streets were alive. You could hear music and smell food from the various food shops on the street. People would speak because everyone either knew you, or knew of you. Now it is a graveyard, a graveyard of lost hopes and dreams of what once was. The pride people had on the street has been replaced with the shame, hopelessness, and despair of drugs and death. No one speaks to you now, because there's a whole new group in town, and something as trivial as a hello could get your throat slit. The smell of barbeque and other food has been replaced with the stench of injustice and hatred for a system that has disenfranchised a people out of their futures and their children. The city as we knew it is gone, gone as if it never existed.

But Nate didn't care, baby Glo was four now and was easily the most spoiled kid I had ever seen. Gabby was known all over as the "big spender". She would go on one-hundred and two-hundred thousand dollar shopping sprees without the bat of neither an eye nor the slightest care. Mike and Dana were the prince and princess of the street, feared and revered county wide. Jon was known all through the criminal world as the "money man," making money for drug men all over the Midwest. The South Side mafia was by now the most brutal group of thugs I had ever laid eyes on; the stories I had heard about their violent escapades would gag a Billy goat. Pete was churning out more powder than Johnson & Johnson, and happy to do it. It gave him a sense of belonging he said. And I...I was the nameless, faceless one that empowered it all through a plethora of contacts, informants, and wannabes that would give us any information that we needed for a price. There were more ministers, cops, and politicians on payroll than I care to remember. Everyone wanted a piece of the pie and a seat at the table, they all wanted to ride.

Since the death of Jackson a couple of years back Nate had silenced all detractors, we didn't believe there were any enemies left, none that counted anyway. We were all enjoying life, traveling and spending our fortunes in any way we chose. Even Dana and Gabby seemed to get along better, we were the kings and queens of the hill, the urban legend that everyone relished. To be in the "family" during those few years was like being in a cross between

Camelot and the Roman Empire. We were all closer knit now; we had developed a kinship and brotherhood that was unrivaled. Nate had succeeded in fulfilling his dream of building the greatest crime family that black folks had ever seen in recent memory. Then…it began to erode.

It has been said that there is a chink in all armor, an end to every road, an Achilles to every great warrior, and a weak link in every chain. The strangest thing though, the things that usually bring down empires was not the thing that destroyed us. Corruption, immorality, and sloppiness didn't do us in, if I can explain it with a simple word I would say the thing that destroyed us was…..boredom. There were no more axes to grind, no more battles to fight and win, no more grudges or vendettas to carry out, things were quiet. We were all rich and bored. Funny thing about money, once you go everywhere you want to go, eat everything you have ever wanted to eat, wear all of the clothes you have ever wanted to wear, drive the cars, sleep with all of the women, what else is left? I remember as a kid I would watch the old show "Lifestyles of the Rich and Famous" with that guy that talked funny. I always wanted to be rich and know what it felt like. I thought a rich man could never get bored. Was I ever wrong! The family had taken trips to the French Riviera, the Caribbean, Africa, Hawaii, everywhere we wanted to go we went. Now, all we do is just sit around eat and get fat. My last fond memory of the family was in '96.

It had been a while since any of us had been anywhere. Nate had been enjoying the White Sox's home games via television. It was now way too dangerous for him to go anywhere near Chicago, so when he wanted to physically see the Sox play he would go see them when they played out of town. It had been rumored that the owner of the Bulls was going to bust up the team if they won the championship at the end of the season, much to the dismay of fans and many of the players. Everyone felt like this would be the last title, so it was kind of historic. The Bulls had three games to two lead in a best of seven game series against the Utah Jazz, and we all knew the Bulls would probably close them out in Utah in game six. Nate came up with the idea of traveling to Utah to see the historic finale. Everyone thought it was a great idea except Gabby. She didn't really care much for basketball being from Columbia and all. She kept talking about how we should get more into football or as we call it here in the States…soccer.

"Don't nobody watch that shit over here girl," Dana snapped.

"They should…it's exciting," Gabriella said with her Bolivian accent.

"What the fuck is so exciting about it? A bunch of motherfuckers running around kicking a checkered ball like some faggots and shit. Then the game lasts like six hours and the damned score is one to nothing! You can have that stupid-ass shit!" Dana said laughing. I didn't want to offend Gabby, but Dana did have a point, the game just never caught on here in the States.

"Fuck you!" Gabby said frustrated.

"Just come with us baby. You don't have to watch the game. You can go shopping or something," Nate said trying to get her to come along.

"In Utah? What the fuck is she gonna by in Utah, Nate? I don't think she's gonna find any Donna Karan up there!" Dana said smiling.

"They got stores and shit up there, she can find something," Mike assured.

"Yeah, baby just come on. I really want you and Glo to come," Nate pleaded. Gabby finally gave in.

The trip was in a few days and everyone was excited and getting ready. I would spend a lot of time with baby Glo who was really getting cute as a little girl. Gabby kept her in the finest clothes and had a beautician come over every other day to do her and the baby's hair. Glo, was fair skinned, with hair almost down her back. She had Nate's big ears that he had as a child, and the cutest dimples. She was truly adorable. And Nate worshipped her, I mean this kid could never do anything wrong. Nate tickled and played with her constantly, he would even play dolls with her. I could tell that he loved her so much, and when things didn't go well with the business or if he was stressed out, he would spend time with her. Sometimes he would just grab her and hold her. I loved playing with her, too, she was a lot of fun.

"Hey uncle G, let's play dolls," Glo said.

"Well, I don't know. I have some work to do in the other room, uh what about later?" She poked her lip out and gave me one of those sad looks as she held the dolls down by her side. "Well ok, let's play then."

Truly she was the most precocious four-year-old I had ever seen. The statements that she made were very advanced for her age. I think it was because of the amount of time she spent with Dana. Often Dana would color with her. Dana liked coloring more than playing with the dolls. I admit it was strange to see Dana laying in the floor coloring with Glo, with a huge gun stuffed in the small of her back.

"Aunty Dana, do you have a boyfriend?" Little Glo asked.

"Well, no why are asking me that girl?" Dana asked as she colored on the page.

"Cause my momma said you don't have a boyfriend, and I told her I believe you did."

"Well tell your mother it's not her business what I have ok?" Dana said slightly agitated.

"It's ok; momma is just saying that because she is jealous, I think," Glo said smiling. But that's just how she was; she had a special place with all of us. At the time she was the only kid in the house so I guess we all had a hand in spoiling her.

Gabby turned out to be a pretty good mom, too. I can't say that I wasn't shocked; she always seemed a little too self-indulgent for anything like motherhood. I guess having a baby changed her for the better.

"Hey G, come into the office, I got somebody here I want you to meet." Nate yelled from out of the office. "G, this is my main man Dee-Lo, Dee, this is my brother G. Dee just got back in town last week. This motherfucker was the best shortstop in the little leagues; we used to be buddies before his mom and pop moved across town."

"Nice to meet you G, Nate has told me all about you," Dee said.

"Nice to meet you, I remember Nate mentioning you from time to time," I replied.

"Dee went to the Marines and did an eight-year stint. They taught him how to blow shit up in there," Nate said making everyone drinks.

"This is a nice-ass place you got here man. I see you've hit the lottery or some shit," Dee said looking around.

"Yeah, something like that. So where did you go while you were in there man?" Nate asked.

"Shit basically just Cali and Germany, then back to Cali. After I discharged, I just pissed around, did odd jobs and shit, then decided to come back here," Dee said.

"Fucking Army, they don't do shit to prepare a motherfucker for the world, just that Army shit," Nate said disgusted.

"Yeah, no shit! So what's up man? You know where I can get a gig or something? I need to work!" Dee asked.

"Nigga, do it look like I been punchin' a fucking clock?" Nate said holding his arms out. "That nine-to-five shit ain't for me dude! But I'll see what I can do for you," Nate said proudly.

I just looked and listened. I really didn't know the guy, but I could feel that Nate trusted him a bit. Glo knocked on the door and gently pushed the door open.

"Daddy, can you play house with me?" Glo asked in her sweet voice.

"Not right now baby. Daddy's got company; where's your mamma at?" Nate asked looking at her with a goofy look on his face. She was really putty in his hands.

"She's asleep, and I can't find Aunty Dana," she said sorrowfully.

"Ok sweety. Go and set everything up and daddy will be in a minute." Glo closed the door and you could hear her running gleefully down the hall.

"*Daddy*, huh? Boy you done went and had a baby girl, huh?" Dee said teasing Nate.

"Yeah man, that's daddy's baby there!" Nate said standing up.

"She's a beautiful girl Nate, and I see she got them big ass ears you had when you was a shorty!" Dee said playfully. Nate playfully gave him the finger and put his drink down and walked out of the room. I really didn't think much of this guy, but I must admit I was interested in his skill for blowing things up.

"So Dee, you know how to blow shit up huh?" I asked.

## Chicago Police Headquarters – 7pm

Trent sat in his office and pondered his life. He thought about the last twenty years, and thought about all of the so-called friends he had made, alliances he had forged and political ties he had knotted. As he sat at his desk drawer, he pulled out a picture of him and some other big shots and brass as they stood on the golf course with then mayor, Richard J Daley. He placed the picture back in the drawer and lit a cigar. Looking around the room of his office he glanced at all of the awards, commendations, trophies, and accolades that spanned a full thirty-five year career with the Chicago Police Department. Much had happened during those years; he had gone from a rookie cop to chief inspector. He had fathered three children and fallen in and out of love at the same time. Trent realized that with as much power as he had garnered, he still was not in control of his life. Somehow there was always someone else to answer to, always something bigger than his dreams and goals. He had always put others' pleasure before his, and now that he has more years behind him than ahead of him, it had made him sick inside. It had made him a hot head, a man with a quick fuse temper, and a giant chip on his shoulder. *What is the meaning of life*, he thought. The only real happiness he had known was with Gloria, and now she was gone.

Thinking back, he wished he had had the guts to make a life with her. But he didn't. It wasn't safe then; it would have cost him too much. But looking back, whatever he was trying to salvage and save, he ended up losing anyway. Power and influence means nothing if you are not happy and true to who you are. A lesson he learned too late in life.

"Harry, you still here?" A detective asked.

"Yeah, just sitting here I guess. I will be leaving in a minute," he said slowly. The young detective looked around the office to catch a glimpse of what Trent was looking at.

"You ok, top?" he asked.

"Yeah, I just wish I could turn back the hands of time, that's all. All I would need is fifteen years," Trent resigned. The detective bowed his head, took a swallow and spoke.

"I heard about what the doctor said – it's not the end of the world though. They diagnosed my uncle ten years ago, and he's healthier now than then, *and* he's cancer free," The young man said encouragingly.

"Hummph, not for me kid. There comes a time in every man's life when he comes full circle. I did that tonight, right here in this office. I lined up all of my triumphs and failures, and I have come to realize that I accomplished a lot, but I lost more. Son, always be true to yourself. Remember that, it'll be all that you have," Trent said looking at the man earnestly. Detective Trent had been diagnosed with prostate cancer that had spread to his bones and pancreas. The doctor gave him about six months to live at the most.

**New Lenox**

Over the next few months I felt an eerie feeling had come over the family. A feeling of impending doom, but on the surface everything was great. The money kept rolling in; we were all enjoying each other and life was good. Still something just wasn't right.

"Hey G, I got another deposit to drop, I need you to go to the cash room with me," Jon said.

As we traveled down the makeshift tunnel to the count and money room I figured I would make conversation with Jon to see if he felt what I felt.

"Don't worry G, everything is all good. Who's gonna come after us? All of our chief enemies are gone."

Still I didn't feel right, so I started to contact some of my intelligence people to see what was on the street. Nothing was going on, but I could feel something wasn't right. The only real enemy we had was the cops, and my sources told me there was nothing in the works as far as an indictment or anything. So I talked to Nate.

"Nah, it's all good G, everything is all love just relax," Nate reassured.

"But Nate that's just it, everything is too calm."

"Ok, who do you think could be after us G?" Nate continued to watch television with his daughter in his lap as he talked.

"I don't know…the police or the Gangster Disciples, maybe?" Nate laughed.

"With the amount of people you have on the street, we would see the cops coming a week before they would get here. And the GD's…they are done. There's not enough of them around to do anything."

According to history, one of the prominent determining factors contributing to the fall of any empire was complacency. The idea that everything is ok; let's eat, drink, and be merry – that's where we were. We were enjoying the fruits of our labor. Nate, our emperor, was becoming more of the family man and less the gangster. Mike and Dana were getting bored without any enemies, and began to get lazy and less aggressive. Jon, our money man, was spending more time with his estranged family in

Orland, however, he still did a great job with the money. Pete kept the drugs going out, but became more detached from the family, too. And Gabriella was busier being a shop-o-holic and drug wife socialite than being a mother, which pissed Nate off to no end. They would argue about it intensely, but it didn't matter Gabby was who she was. Most of little Glo's time was spent with Nate, which made them even closer. With everyone fat and happy – so to speak – it was my job to make sure things didn't slip, so I talked with Nate and the others about it at breakfast one morning.

"Hey what if we suddenly had to leave this house, where would we go and how would we escape?" I asked everyone.

"Well we have safe houses all over the city and suburbs G. There are a lot of places we could go," Nate said as he sipped coffee.

"No, I mean what would be our escape plan, and do we even have one?"

"No, I don't think we do, and that's a good point. Let me think about that and get back to you G," Nate said as he picked up the paper from the table to begin to read. But the old Nate would have been on top of it before I had mentioned it.

"Hey Nate, I heard Trent is in the hospital with only a few weeks left; he got cancer and shit," Mike said with a half smile.

"Yeah, I heard…couldn't have happened to a nicer guy," Nate said with a sly grin.

"Nate, Trent is a cool dude…you shouldn't wish that on anybody. Plus he was good to Mamma Williams and us years back," I argued.

"I don't see him shedding any tears over my mamma. When she died, that motherfucker just got right back to his old life like she never existed," Nate snapped back.

"Yeah, but damn Nate, the guy is dying now. Can't you let some of that shit go?"

"Fuck him!" Nate said flatly.

After some small talk and Dana telling us all she was going upstate to see her sister in the mental facility, I decided to sneak and see Trent at the hospital that night to pay some sort of respect. Just as we began to finish Gabby announced that she was going shopping and needed Nate to watch Glo for her.

"Not this time, you know you are a mother. I never see you with the baby; you need to be more of a mother and stay out of those fucking stores!" Nate said.

"Nate please, I'm just asking you to do this once. I will be back in an hour or so," Gabby said.

"Bullshit, your hour or so turns into four fucking hours. Dana spends more time with the kid than you do!" Nate said angrily. Gabby slammed her fork down wiped her mouth and left the table abruptly. "And don't leave her with the help staff either!" Nate shouted.

"Well, I better start heading upstate. You guys know how to reach me if you need to," Dana said leaving the table.

"Hey hook up with me later Dana; we got some running around to do. Also, Nate," Mike said as he and Pete left also.

"Call me Mike! You know we got that meeting later tonight with Jon and our people," Nate yelled. After everyone left I gave Nate a long look, he could tell I wanted to talk. "What G? What is it?" Nate said sarcastically.

"You ok? Are you alright?" I asked.

"Yeah, I just hate a lot of stupid shit. She never spends time with Glo you know, I ain't used to that type of shit G. Mamma spent time with us…you know playing games and shit. This one here is always in these fucking stores, which I have warned her about repeatedly," Nate said in disgust.

"Gabby is what she is Nate. You can't make her mamma. She's a free spirit; she just ain't the mothering type. You knew that four years ago," I reasoned.

"Yeah, if I had known then what I know now, I probably would have left her ass in that fucking rain forest!" Nate said.

"Then you wouldn't have Glo."

"Yeah, that's right. I guess I got something out of the deal," Nate said smiling. I wiped my mouth and started to rise up before Nate stopped me.

"G, what do we do now?" he asked in sorrowful reflect.

"I don't know Nate, I honestly don't know." I said humbly.

The problem with being "in the life" is that once you have established yourself, gotten rid of or made peace with your enemies, enjoyed your money, there's nothing left. You've done everything, seen everything, and experienced everything. Then you begin to find out that life is more than sex, drugs, cars, clothes, and money. You begin to realize there is a deeper meaning to life. But by then it doesn't matter; you have already sold your soul; all you can do now is wait for your fate……jail or the grave. Every drug kingpin knows that feeling. He knows the feeling of not being able to trust anyone, the feeling of impending doom, the feeling of death slow-walking you down. Because Dr. King was right, 'the arc of the moral universe is low, but it bends toward justice.' The bible is right 'Every man will reap what he has sown.' These feelings are benign in the beginning. It is when your grave is dug, your fate is sealed when the malignancy of the situation kicks in, then it is too late. In the beginning everyone is along for the ride, but when it is time to pay the piper you stand alone. It is at this time that the ghosts of all those you have murdered begin to haunt you. It is at this time that you start to have trouble sleeping; it is at this time when you are labeled by all of your peers as "paranoid". It is at this time when you begin to ask your closest confidants "What do we do now"? Nate was at the threshold of the end and he could sense it; the sad part was he couldn't stop it. Of course every drug boy swears his story will end differently, yet he cannot name one in history that has. I believe if every gangster or drug dealer could speak from the grave they would all attest to the fact that the end never justifies the means.

Later that night I took a couple of mafia guys with me into the city to visit Trent at the hospital. Gabby and Glo had not returned yet and I figured when she did, she and Nate would be fighting and I didn't want to stick around for that shit. During the ride I thought about what I would say to him. Hell I hadn't seen him in years and was not sure if he would recognize me. I knew a guy that worked in housekeeping at Northwestern Hospital and he agreed to get me in after visiting hours. He worked it out with Trent's nurse so everything was cool.

"Look the nurse said, 'don't stay long'…he's on morphine so he might not say much or recognize you. He's really in bad shape, man. His family just left about an hour ago so everything's cool," the young man said.

As I walked into the room at first glance I didn't recognize him. He had lost so much weight and he looked dried up and white as a sheet. I grabbed a chair and sat next to him quietly.  Maybe I will just sit here for a minute and leave, I just felt weird.  Then he turned to face me and opened his eyes.

"Derrick….how….how are you?  It's been a….long time," he said weakly in between coughs.

"Uh…I've been ok detective, I just came to uh, see you.  Is there anything I can get you?"

"No, I was…..praying you would…come."

"Well your prayers were answered," I said half smiling.  He took a deep swallow and looked straight up into the ceiling.

"You know…..Gloria died in this….room.   I requested it you know…I requested this ….room.  I miss her so…much.   She is the only….woman I have…ever loved, I know….that now," he said as a tear welled up in his eye.  I wished Nate could have heard him say that, maybe his feelings about him would have changed.  Then I had to ask him why he didn't marry her, I had to know that.  "Stupid…stupid and scared," he managed to say.  "Listen….Derrick; I have something to tell you," he said trying to muster strength he didn't have.  "They...they're gonna come...after you boys.  It is…..good that you came…you were the smartest one.  Nathan is.tough but he….he leads with his…..emotions like his mother...and this is….life and death."

"Who?  Detective, who is 'they'?"  I asked as I scooted closer to his face to hear him better.  He gave me a long look as he squinted his eyes.

"He…didn't tell…..you?" he said with a slight smile.

"Tell me what detective.   You're not making sense," I said in a loud whisper as not to be heard.

"There's not much time. Listen to me, they know where you all are. They...they're gonna kill you, boys. You've got to get out of that house," Trent said.

"Ok, how long do we have, do you know?" I asked frantically.

"Not long. A week or two, maybe? Go....go save him, Derrick. I promised Gloria...," he said before fading out from the pain medication.

Then it hit me. I got up and walked briskly to the door and turned back to look at Trent one last time. I knew it would be the last time I would see him alive. In the car it all made sense...sort of. I didn't know the "who's" or any of the specifics, but I had always suspected a third party in all of this, but who was it? My head was spinning as the truck sped down I57, and onto I80 west. I had to get to Nate soon to get some answers. Then I remembered I couldn't talk to Nate about it because I wasn't supposed to be going to see Trent in the first place. This was important though, maybe someone else could help me. As the truck circled the long drive way before stopping at the door, I remembered pulling my gun out and cocking it while looking around. I don't know what the hell I was going to do. I hadn't shot anybody before. I guess it was just blind instinct. The first person I saw was Pete, and he looked flustered about something.

"What's up Pete?" I asked concerned.

"Hey man bad news. Gabby and the baby were in a car accident. Nate is upstairs going off looking for you, and he said you didn't answer your phone. He said he was on his way to the city to the hospital," Pete said.

"He can't go to the city, it's too dangerous," I said anxiously.

"G! Where the fuck have you been, man? I been calling all over the fucking city for you're ass!" Nate yelled from the top of the stairs.

"I was on some business Nate! I didn't hear...,"

"Fuck that. The baby and Gabby have been in a car accident. I'm going to the hospital to see how they are doing!" he said scampering down the spiral staircase putting on his jacket.

"Nate maybe you better let me and Mike go. It's way too dangerous for you to be seen out there."

"Fuck that shit. My baby is out there...that's my baby, G. I don't give a fuck about that bullshit you talking!" he yelled.

"Nate, just listen to me. If you go out there, you might be spotted. I need to talk to you about some shit before you go just running out there! Let's just reason for a minute!" I said emphatically.

"Man fuck that!! he said as he shoved past me. I signaled for some mafia guys to go with him and instructed Mike to trail them. By the time Mike got to his truck, Nate had gotten into Dana's Corvette and drove off without any bodyguards.

"Catch his ass and trail him, better yet I'll go, too. Where is Jon?" I asked.

"Shit I don't know...we ain't seen him all day," Mike said. We were able to catch up to Nate on the Dan Ryan. If it had not been for a traffic stall, we wouldn't have caught him especially in that Corvette. While in the car I asked Mike about what Trent told me to see if he knew anything.

"I don't know shit about that G. All I know is Jon and Nate go to meet some people every other month or so. And they never take anyone with them," Mike said. Of course Dana knew nothing either, the only person I thought might know something was Jon and he had strangely disappeared. Strangely Glo and Gabby were at Northwestern too. Glo was in intensive care and was soon to be rushed to Children's Memorial. When we arrived Nate told us what had happened. Some car had tried to run them off the road intentionally according to an eyewitness. Gabby suffered extensive head injuries and little Glo had suffered facial cuts and also some head injuries. Nate was outdone; I hadn't seen him like this since the death of Mamma Williams. I had Mike and a couple of the mafia guys go and undo whatever Nate had done in his emotional frenzy. I went into the waiting room and Nate was sitting with his arms folded and his feet crossed at the ankles and was rocking intensely back and forth. Dana stood over him rubbing his head and trying to console him. The doctor came in and told us that Gabby had been taken to emergency surgery to relieve the pressure from her brain. He instructed us that her chances were not good.

"What about my baby…how is she?"

"She is being air lifted to Children's Memorial. They will do all that they are able to do; they have the best staff there for these situations Mr.…," the doctor said fishing for Nate's name.

"Anderson…Ron Anderson. Look we are going to send some people to Children's. Can you make sure that they are met without any confusion or problems sir?" I asked.

"Sure, I will alert them that you will be coming, are you related to the baby?" he asked.

"I am her uncle and these are relatives, also," I explained. I noticed a cop was coming down the hall; he was a ways off so we had time to get out.

"Nate, look the cops are coming…probably to get a statement. We've got to get out of here. Maybe we can get to Children's," I said hurriedly. Nate nodded his head in agreement with tears streaming down his face.

"Doctor these men will stay," I said. I then turned to Mike and the mafia guys and instructed them to call me as soon as there was word about Gabby and we left. During the whole ride to Lincoln Park, Nate never said a word. He just kept rocking and wringing his hands together. Of course Glo and the helicopter beat us to Children's and when we got there, they had already started working on her. By now I had managed to calm Nate down and get a cup of coffee into him.

"What I really need is a drink," he smiled nervously. Nate went to the bathroom and I sent a couple of the mafia guys with him. As soon as they left, my phone rang.

"Yeah, talk to me," I said quickly.

"She's gone….she died in surgery. We are on our way there," Mike said and then hung up the phone. I slapped my phone shut in disgust. *How was I gonna tell Nate this?* I told Dana to try to call Hugo in Bolivia. When we got home on the secure line and try to get in touch with Gabby's mother and family. Nate came down the hall and he looked at me and knew from the look on my face what had happened.

"Which one?" he shouted.

"Gabby. She's gone Nate. She died in surgery," I said calmly. Nate threw his arms around my neck and started to ball like a baby. The woman he had met and fell for half a world away, the mother of his first born child was dead. Gabby and Nate had their differences, but I never doubted his love for her. I really felt sorry for him, the rest of us just tried to be there for him. Even Dana shed a tear for Gabby and admitted that she would miss her. We didn't get a chance to mourn Gabby long before the news about Glo came back. She had made it through surgery, but had slipped into a coma because of the loss of blood. The doctor instructed that the next 48 hours were critical. Nate made up his mind that he would stay the entire 48 hours until she changed for the better. The others were instructed to go home and wait for our call.

Nate went down to the gift shop, purchased about fifteen children's books, and said he would read to her because she liked that. I had so much going on in my head I thought it would burst: so many questions, so many things I had to know. I dared not mention them now. It just wasn't the right time. *And where in the fuck was Jon*, I thought.

"Hey look I'm gonna stay here with Nate for the night at least, go home and try to find Jon. If he is alive and breathing get his ass down here immediately!" I instructed Mike and Dana.

We waited until little Glo was in her room and we went up there to sit with her. She looked so pitiful. She was so full of life, so sweet, it broke my heart to see her laying there with tubes, and machines hooked up to her little body. Nate started to sob when he saw her.

"My sweet baby…look what they did to my sweet baby," he sobbed. I tried to remain strong, to be the rock he needed at this time. *Who could do this to a child and mother?* We stood about eight feet from her and Nate started wiping his face and blowing his nose. "Fix yourself up G, I don't want her to see us crying." He went over to her bedside and laid the books on the table. "Hello sweetie, daddy and G are here. I know you aren't feeling well, but we are gonna read to you for a while until you get better. Everything is gonna be all right. I'm gonna stay right here until you wake up. You're just tired, that's all and you need a little sleep," Nate said adjusting her hair and pulling out her favorite book, *Green Eggs and Ham*. Nate looked exhausted; he really needed some sleep.

I guess he was just running on adrenaline or something. After about four hours of reading, I noticed I had nodded off, and it was close to three in the morning. Nate was still reading, he hadn't missed a beat! Dana called me on the phone and told me that there was still no word from Jon. She asked me if I thought he had flipped and turned state on us. I didn't think so, although it was weird that he hadn't been found. I sincerely thought he had taken a shit load of money and his kid and left the country. That was more like Jon. Nate had taken a break and came to talk to me about the phone call.

"Any word on Jon yet?" Nate asked.

"Nothing…I don't understand. It's not like him to do this. It's weird," I stated in bewilderment.

"Yeah. Well tell them when they find him, kill him," Nate said as he walked over to begin reading to Glo again. He kneeled down and picked up the next book to begin.

"Hey Nate you're tired man. We can't do anymore here for Glo. She is in good care. Maybe we should go home, get a shower, and a good night's sleep and come back in the morning, huh?" I asked touching him on the arm. He gave me a very mean look and jerked his arm away from me and started back reading. I didn't know what to do, so I went back over to my chair and went to sleep.

Early the next morning I was awakened by the vibration of my phone.

"Hello?"

"Yeah man…still no word on Jon. How's Nate doing?" the voice asked. It was Pete.

"Shit, he's asleep next to Glo. I'd better get him up. How is everything there?" I asked.

"Good, maybe you guys should come home and get some real sleep," Pete said.

"I want to, but Nate won't have it and I ain't leaving him out here by himself."

"Well try to talk him into it. We are gonna eat and get cleaned up and come out there to get you guys," Pete said before hanging up. I closed my phone and proceeded to go and wake up Nate. We needed to get home.

"Shit what time is it?" he asked.

"It's almost nine thirty in the morning, man," I replied.

"Did she wake up yet?" he asked hopefully.

"I don't think so Nate. She probably will later tonight," I said trying to instill hope.

"Yeah, you're probably right."

"Look, I'm gonna go downstairs to the gift shop and get us some toothbrushes and some soap and shit before someone comes in here. We probably smell like billy goats!" I said trying to lighten the mood.

"Humph, yeah that's probably a good idea."

All the way down I tried to put some of this stuff together and watch my back at the same time. I truly hated living this way. Maybe it was time for us to take a shit load of money and leave the country, but with Glo being in this shape, Nate wouldn't even entertain the thought. When I got back upstairs the neurosurgeon was in the room talking to Nate.

"Everything is still the same as yesterday, but she is in good hands, sir. Maybe you should go home and get some sleep and come back tonight," he advised.

"Yeah, they're taking good care of her. Let's go get some sleep," I said entering the room. Nate took a long look at her and let out a deep sigh.

"Ok, but I will be right back tonight baby," he said kissing her on the forehead. After the doctor left Nate went in and washed up. While he was in there I called Mike and Dana again.

"Anything yet?" I asked.

"Nothing, that motherfucker is gone. I ain't even looking for him anymore. He's either dead or gone, that's it," Dana said disgusted.

"Yeah, well you all hurry up and get down here. I've talked him into coming home," I said as I slapped the phone shut. I was really worried. Not about Jon, but about our next move. I couldn't figure out who was after us, but I had narrowed it down to three entities: the cops, Gangster Disciples, or this strange hidden hand. But it couldn't be the Gangster Disciples, there weren't enough of them left to do anything to anybody, plus how would Trent know what they were going to do. Maybe the hidden hand was the cops, but why would they try and kill us? Maybe Nate made a deal with them and tried to cut them out or something? Maybe Trent was just talking out of his head, but he seemed so sincere? Also, who would try and run Gabby and the baby off the road? Cops don't do that shit. It had to be some rogue outfit or something. I came to one conclusion…Mike and Dana would have to be my gauge. If it was some sort of authoritative set, if it was the local cops, or some sort of federal unit like the FBI or ATF guys, they would probably arrest Nate and I first. But if they killed Mike and Dana first then my worst fears would be realized. Whoever it was, I was pretty sure at this point that they had Jon. The worst thing was, all I could do was wait. With Glo being sick, Nate and I running was totally out of the question.

Once we got home I had to sit down with Mike and Dana and go over everything. They seemed calm about the whole situation, but they were sure that Jon was dead.

"He wouldn't rat us out. That ain't Jon," Mike said in his defense.

"Shit I don't know. It's a funny business we are in, anything is possible," Pete said.

"Yeah, well if he ain't dead, he may as well be," Dana said sternly.

"G, God forbid, but what do we do if Glo dies?" Mike asked.

"If little Glo dies, then we get the fuck out of here as soon as possible. I don't know who is after us but we can't take any chances," I cautioned.

"Man that motherfucker Trent was on morphine. Shit he probably didn't even know who the fuck he was talking to," Dana said.

"Maybe, but what if he wasn't? This is our lives we are talking about here. We can't take unnecessary chances. So until then everybody better stay in the house. Mike, Dana get your regimes on high alert. If we get raided, we will let the soldiers fight. We will escape through the tunnel downstairs. I talked to that guy Nate knows a week or so ago. I got the whole house rigged with C4 and a matrix switch that will detonate it from at least a thousand yards away. Once we are clear we will blow this fucker along with all of the evidence to kingdom come," I instructed.

"That's it, that's your plan?" Dana asked incredulously.

"Well if anyone can come up with anything else I am open," I said.

"Shit I don't think it's gonna come down to that G, plus we can't just blow up millions of dollars. And what about the service staff and all of the brothers in the regime? We just blow all of them up too?" Mike asked. I didn't say a word, I just looked at them as if I couldn't believe they were asking me that.

"That's my plan, and everyone stays put until I can figure this shit out," I said finally. It was noon now and starting to rain outside. Nate was still asleep. He was as obviously exhausted as I was, but I couldn't sleep. I kept thinking about our situation, and what we would do. Then the hospital called. The nurse told me that Glo had died in her sleep; they had tried to revive her but it wasn't to be. I guess her little body couldn't take the whole situation and gave out. At least that was my understanding. The official cause of death was "brain seizures" whatever that was. Our little Glo was gone. I told Mike, Dana, and Pete. Immediately they started to cry. We all hugged each other and I took one of the longest walks in my life upstairs to tell her father. I didn't know how he was going to react. I walked past those devilish dogs of his without even noticing they were there. I opened the French doors to his room and saw him sprawled across the bed sleeping. I just stood there and sniffled as tears streamed down my face. I guess he heard me and looked up.

"Damn you scared the shit out of me," he said as he looked at his watch. He didn't notice my tears because of the darkness of the room. Nate was notorious for keeping the shades pulled; he always felt someone would be watching him sleep or something. "Shit G, it's almost one-thirty, why the hell didn't you wake me up? I gotta get to the hospital," he said as he jumped off the bed and scampered around the room looking for his pants. "G, don't just stand there man get your ass ready. We gotta go!" He said still not looking up at me. He finally looked at me and saw the expression on my face and he knew. "G I told you to wake me! I told you to wake me! I wanted to be there! My baby! You motherfucker, I told you to let me know!" He screamed as he fell to the floor with one leg in his pants and one leg out. I walked over to the bed and kneeled down and hugged him. Nate let out a scream into my chest that had to have been heard a block away. Mike and Dana came running up the stairs with their guns drawn. After seeing us they put them away and I heard Dana sobbing as Mike walked her out of the room.

Glo was the only innocent thing in our family. She was not just Nate and Gabby's baby, she was all of ours, and we all loved her. Raw emotion filled the house as we all spent the rest of the day sobbing and mourning. I made some calls to the funeral parlor and some preachers we knew and arranged a private ceremony a few days later for Gabby and Glo. Nate wanted Gabby's body flown back to Bolivia. He felt Gabby should be buried with her people in her native country. Besides Gabby didn't know anyone here except us and her mother was distraught about her death. Nate confided to me that he felt the worst for her mother. He had promised to take care of Gabby and now he had to send her back to her mother in a coffin. The guilt of Gabby and Glo was ripping him apart. He felt it was his lifestyle that killed his family. He felt that he put them in harm's way, by living the way he did.

After their memorial services, he went into a depression. Drinking and smoking reefer was the only thing that put him to sleep at night. He didn't shave or bathe for that matter. I was pretty much running things. I didn't mind; I just wanted to keep my brother from losing his mind. After all, he was all the family that I had left. About a week after everything was over, I had let my guard down. The money kept coming in and I had forgotten about the whole Trent warning and all. I was too busy looking after Nate. The house seemed so empty now that they were gone. Nate said that his insides ached all the time after them. By now he had a full unkempt beard and he walked around all of the time drunk and/or high. I don't even think he showered three times a week. Nobody ever heard from Jon again, and we were beginning to plan out how we were gonna get things back in order again as far as Nate.

"Maybe we should get him some help; I mean professional G," Pete said drinking his club soda.

"I thought about that Pete, but who? I don't know anyone like that, plus it has to be somebody I would be able to trust," I said.

"We don't have any choice G. Nate's going down the tubes; we have to get him some help now," Dana said.

"Let's go get something to eat. I'm hungry," Mike said.

"What are you guys getting?" I asked.

"Probably Harold's," Dana said.

"Count me out. I can't eat that heavy this late at night. But look you guys be careful ok?" I warned.

"G, you worry too much relax baby," Dana said kissing me on the forehead.

"Get your coat Pete. We'll take Pete with us," Mike said.

"What about taking some mafia guys with you too?" I asked.

"Nah, we don't need an entourage to get chicken," Dana said. After they left out I sent some guys to trail them anyway. After they left I went upstairs to check on Nate. He was curled up in his bed in the fetal position with a bag of weed and a bottle of cognac on his nightstand. I walked over and checked him out and covered him with a blanket. I decided I would get some staff to clean up his room in the morning as I looked around. When I got into the room, I figured a glass of Cognac might not be a bad idea; it probably would help me sleep too.


**Country Club Hills, IL**
"Why did you take this big-ass truck tonight just to go get some chicken?" Dana asked.

"Shit I like my truck. It don't make any difference, you ain't driving!" Mike snapped back. Dana looked in the rear view mirror and noticed Pete sleeping.

"Wake your ass up nigga, you supposed to be watching our back, and you're back there sleep!" she said. Pete gave her the finger and went back to sleep. "What you want nigga?" Dana asked him.

"Nothing, I don't eat that type shit at night," Pete said barely opening his eyes.

"Fuck you then. What you getting?" she said looking at Mike.

"I'm going in, I think I want something different tonight," Mike said as he opened the truck door. Dana got out and stretched and tucked a huge gun into her back.

"We outta look into getting one of these in Lenox, so we won't have to drive all the way out her for some chicken," she said.

"I don't think they eat Harold's in New Lenox baby. This fucking parking lot is so damned dark. Pete keep your fucking eyes open nigga," Mike said knocking on the window. Mike put on his huge leather jacket over his massive frame and he and Dana started walking toward the strip mall and into the restaurant. As they walked in, two men got out of an unmarked vehicle dressed in black from head to toe with automatic assault rifles and scurried across the lot and positioned themselves under the belly of the huge SUV.

"What you getting?" Dana asked Mike.

"Probably just a half white...I think I'm gonna stick with what I know baby," Mike said rubbing his chin. After making and receiving their orders, the two walked out of the restaurant and toward the SUV.

"It's gonna rain, I can smell it in the air," Dana said looking up at the dark sky.

"Probably so. I gotta make sure those cars are washed tomorrow. I used to let little Glo sit out with me while they were being washed," Mike said reflecting as he opened the door. Dana let out a sigh and hopped into the truck.

"This motherfucker still sleep. Pete wake your ass up...," Dana shouted as she noticed two men standing about nine feet away from the truck with masks on. The men that had crawled under the truck waited until Mike and Dana were in and crawled out and positioned themselves for fire.

"Mike, it's a Hit!" Dana shouted. Dana and Mike reached for their guns, but it was too late. The two men fired at least seventy to eighty rounds into the truck as both tires were shot to flat and all of the windows exploded from the gunfire. Dana made a vain effort at getting out of the car, but fell helpless as half of her bullet riddled body lay half out of the side of the truck. The two men ended their gunfire and walked over to make sure all parties were dead. As they walked over toward Dana's half dead body, they noticed that she was still moaning, but barely alive. One of the masked men quickly pulled out a handgun and ended her pain by shooting her in the head. Both men chuckled as they walked toward the unmarked vehicle they had arrived in. One of he men noticed two mafia guys running to get back into their vehicles and ran toward the men.

## New Lenox

I remember pouring myself a glass of cognac and walking toward the remote and turning on the television. I always made it a habit of watching CNN news to see what was going on in the world. This night tuning in may have saved my life. There was breaking news that an early morning raid onto the compound of a reputed drug czar who had ties to the Columbian drug cartel Hugo Zamora had been gunned down. Further, many of his followers were taken into custody by US and Columbian drug officials. Many eyewitnesses and some local police officials had stated that Hugo was killed in the raid. To say that I was outdone was an understatement. Before I could get my thoughts together the phone rang. I picked it up and answered it reluctantly.

"Boss....Boss...we are being chased by some guys. They....they killed Dana, and Mike and Pete! Get out of there now!" The frantic voice screamed before it was silenced by automatic gunfire. My heart immediately started pounding from adrenaline as I dropped my glass of cognac on the floor and started running up the spiral staircase to get Nate. I found a mafia bodyguard on the way up and told him to help me. As I ran up the stairs toward Nate's room I saw his demonic dogs jump to attention from my running up the stairs so frantically. I remembered the gun in the small of my back, drew it and shot both dogs before I got to the top of the staircase. I kicked open the door and threw the covers back and told the mafia guy to pick up Nate and carry him downstairs. I picked up Nate's pants and pulled out his wallet and threw it on the floor. Mafia guys were starting out of their rooms from the sound of the gunfire. I told them that we were being raided and to get their body armor on and take cover to protect the house. Then I ran into my room in a panic and picked up a large suitcase with about one million cash in it and the matrix switch I had manufactured by Nate's friend, Dee. I reached into my back pocket and threw my wallet on the floor and shot back out of the room. I leaped down the stairs skipping about four or five at a time and met the mafia guy and Nate at the bottom of the stairs.

  I flung open the door and told him to follow me. We ran to the driveway straight to Gabby's old Bentley. I flung open the back door and told the mafia guy to put Nate in the back. I opened the driver's side and threw the suitcase into the passenger side and quickly closed the door. I stood up and intentionally dropped my keys on the ground near the mafia underling and instructed him to hand them to me. When he bent over to pick them up I shot him in the back of the head as not to be seen. I kicked him over and hopped into the car and started the engine. I turned on the remote switch and waited for the green signal. I remember driving down the winding driveway and promising myself to run over anyone that happened to get in my way. I was now sweating profusely and nervous because I knew that whoever it was that killed Mike and Dana were on their way to get us. Time was of the essence! I remember there was a safe house that only Nate and I knew about around ten miles west of New Lenox. My plan was to get there and wake Nate up and clear my head as to our next move. Once the remote switch hit green, I hit the detonator switch and as I got onto the main street in front of the compound I heard what sounded like a nuclear explosion. I had about one hundred pounds of C4 connected to the foundation of the house and asked Dee to set it to go off after I would be clear of the blast, which he said probably would be about one hundred feet or so.

I knew that by blowing up the house I would be killing all of the service staff and most of the mafia guys from both regimes, but I didn't care, as long as Nate and I escaped alive. That night I murdered at least eighty people living in and near the main house. I remember trying to calm myself down to do the speed limit so I wouldn't get pulled over. I was so nervous I was shaking. I remember thinking that I should probably just keep going to the Mexican border or something, but that would be ridiculous. I had to think of a way out of the situation. I hated night driving; to tell the truth I really wasn't an experienced driver. I learned at eighteen and soon after we got into the drug game and I was pretty much driven around all of the time. I started to calm down once I knew we had gotten away and weren't being followed. The trouble was the calmer I got, the sleepier I became. I remember looking back at Nate and he was snoring pretty loud. *Fucking idiot*, I thought. He doesn't even know what's going on. My mind started wandering as I drove down the black highway. *What a fucking day!* This morning when we got up for breakfast, all of the people who were important in me and Nate's life were alive and well. And now here I was driving down I80 at three in the morning and everyone was dead. We lost so many and so much in such a short time. Nancy Wilson once sang a song entitled "What a difference a day makes". Ain't that the fucking truth! Yesterday Nate and I were secure and rich; now we were on the run with nowhere to go. All the money and stuff didn't matter. Our friends both near and far were dead. I remember yawning for about the fourth time in ten minutes and felt myself getting sleepier. I rolled down the windows and turned up the music loud. The road was so dark and the lines on the road were starting to run together. I realized I was dozing off. I immediately shook my head and tried to collect myself. *Boy If I could just get thirty minutes of sleep I could drive one hundred miles.*

Then I started to think about Hugo and who might have set him up. *How did they know about us here in the States?* It had to be some government shit to be able to reach halfway around the world. I remember feeling so exhausted as my eyes closed again, this time for at least fifteen seconds. Long enough to be awakened by someone blowing at me and seeing myself running off the road! I tried to steer back but I lost control of the vehicle and drove into the embankment off the shoulder. I remember hitting my head and face on the steering wheel and crashing the car. The car rolled over onto the driver's side and slid a few feet and stopped. I remember being semi-conscious and trying to call Nate.

"Hey man.....you.....ok?" I asked feeling groggy. I heard Nate groan and a car stop behind us. I tried to stay conscious knowing that if I didn't, we would probably wake up in a hospital chained to a bed in custody.

"Are you guys ok? Go call an ambulance!" I heard a man say just before I fell out of consciousness.

**NEGLECTED SOULS**

Motherhood and the trials of loving too hard and not enough
frame this story...The realism of these characters will bring
tears to your spirit as you discover the hero in the villain you
never saw coming...

Neglected Souls is a gritty, honest and heart-stirring story of
hope and personal triumph set in the ghettos of Boston.

**In Stores!!!**

Jimmy and Nina continue to feel a void in their lives because they haven't a clue about their genealogical make-up. Jimmy falls victims to a life threatening illness and only the right organ donor can save his life. Will the donor be the bridge to reconnect Jimmy and Nina to their biological family? Will Nina be the strength for her brother in his time of need? Will they ever find out what really happened to their mother?

**In Stores!!!**

Betrayal, lust, lies, murder, deception, sex and tainted love frame
this story... Julian Stevens lacks the ambition and freak ability that
Miko looks for in a man, but she married him despite his flaws to
spite an ex-boyfriend. When Miko least expects it, the old
boyfriend shows up and ready to sweep her off her feet again.
Suddenly the grass grows greener on the other side, but Miko is not
an easily satisfied woman. She wants to have her cake and eat it
too. While Miko's doing her own thing, Julian is determined to
become everything Miko ever wanted in a man and more, but will
he go to extreme lengths to prove he's worthy of Miko's love? Julian
Stevens soon finds out that he's capable of being more than he
could ever imagine as he embarks on a journey that will change his
life forever.

**In Stores!!**

The police in New York and other major cities around the country are increasingly victimizing black men. The violence has escalated to deadly force, most of the time without justification. In this controversial book, noted author Richard Jeanty, tackles the problem of police brutality and the unfair treatment of Black men at the hands of police in New York City and the rest of the country. The conflict between the Police and Black men will continue on a downward spiral until the mayors of every city hold accountable the members of their police force who use unnecessary deadly force against unarmed victims.

## In Stores!!!

Just when Darren thinks his relationship with Tina is
flourishing, there is yet another hurdle on the road hindering
their bliss. Tina saw a therapist for months to deal with her
sexual addiction, but now Darren is wondering if she was
ever treated completely. Darren has not been taking care of
home and Tina's frustrated and agrees to a break-up with
Darren. Will Darren lose Tina for good? Will Tina ever
realize that Darren is the best man for her?

**In Stores!!**

Ronald Murphy was a player all his life until he and his best friend, Myles, met the women of their dreams during a brief vacation in South Beach, Florida. Sexual Jeopardy is story of trust, betrayal, forgiveness, friendship, hope and HIV.

**In Stores!!!**

Tina develops an insatiable sexual appetite very early in life. She only loves her boyfriend, Darren, but he's too far away in college to satisfy her sexual needs.

Tina decides to get buck wild away in college

Will her sexual trysts jeopardize the lives of the men in her life?

**In Stores!!!**

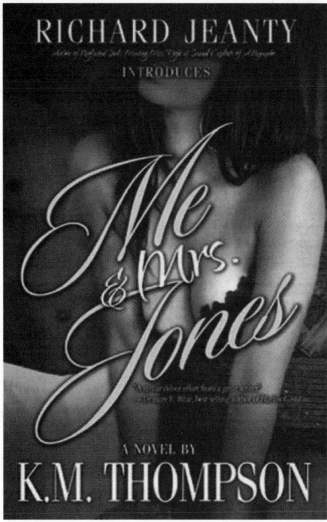

RICHARD JEANTY

INTRODUCES

*Me & Mrs. Jones*

A NOVEL BY

K.M. THOMPSON

Faith Jones, a woman in her mid-thirties, has given up on ever finding love again until she met her son's best friend, Darius. Faith Jones is walking a thin line of betrayal against her son for the love of Darius. Will Faith allow her emotions to outweigh her common sense?

**In Stores!!!**

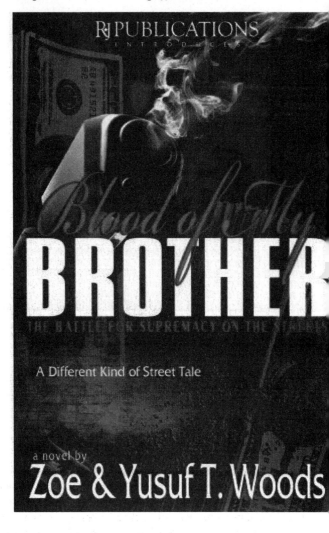

Roc was the man on the streets of Philadelphia, until his younger brother decided it was time to become his own man by wreaking havoc on Roc's crew without any regards for the blood relation they share. Drug, murder, mayhem and the pursuit of happiness can lead to deadly consequences. This story can only be told by a person who has lived it.

**In Stores!!!**

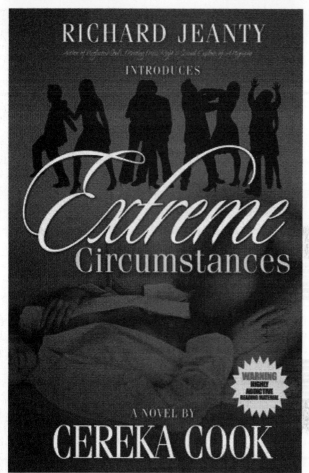

RICHARD JEANTY

INTRODUCES

*Extreme*
Circumstances

A NOVEL BY
CEREKA COOK

What happens when a devoted woman is betrayed? Come
take a ride with Chanel as she takes her boyfriend, Donnell,
to circumstances beyond belief after he betrays her trust with
his endless infidelities. How long can Chanel's friend, Janai,
use her looks to get what she wants from men before it
catches up to her? Find out as Janai's gold-digging ways
catch up with and she has to face the consequences of her
extreme actions.

**In Stores!!!**

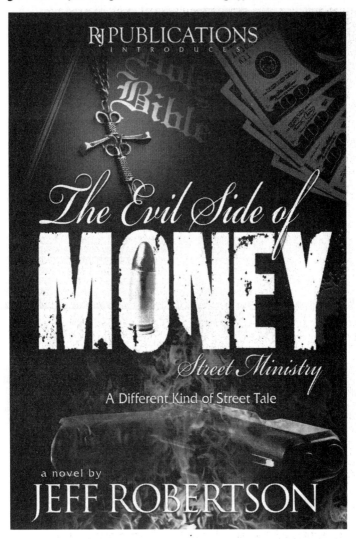

RJ PUBLICATIONS
INTRODUCES

The Evil Side of

# MONEY

*Street Ministry*

A Different Kind of Street Tale

a novel by

## JEFF ROBERTSON

Violence, Intimidation and carnage are the order as Nathan
and his brother set out to build the most powerful drug
empires in Chicago. However, when God comes knocking,
Nathan's conscience starts to surface. Will his haunted
criminal past get the best of him?

**In Stores!!**

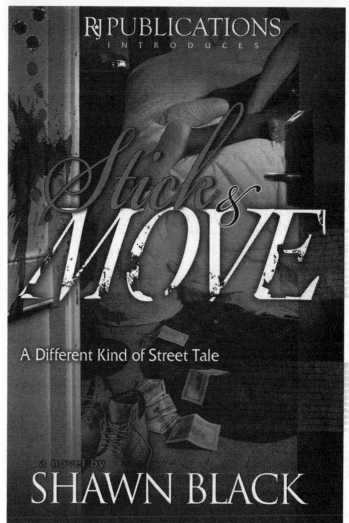

RJ PUBLICATIONS
INTRODUCES

*Stick & MOVE*

A Different Kind of Street Tale

a novel by
SHAWN BLACK

Yasmina witnessed the brutal murder of her parents at a young age at the hand of a drug dealer. This event stained her mind and upbringing as a result. Will Yamina's life come full circle with her past? Find out as Yasmina's crew, The Platinum Chicks, set out to make a name for themselves on the street.

**In stores!!**

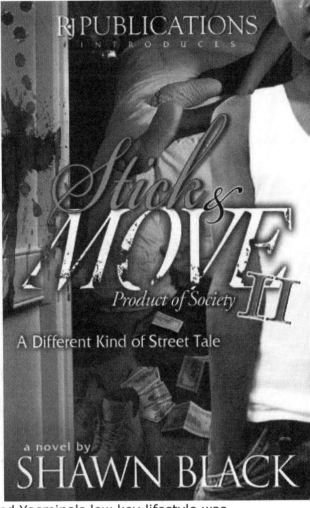

Scorcher and Yasmina's low key lifestyle was interrupted when they were taken down by the Feds, but their daughter, Serosa, was left to be raised by the foster care system. Will Serosa become a product of her environment or will she rise above it all? Her bloodline is undeniable, but will she be able to control it?

**Coming soon!!**

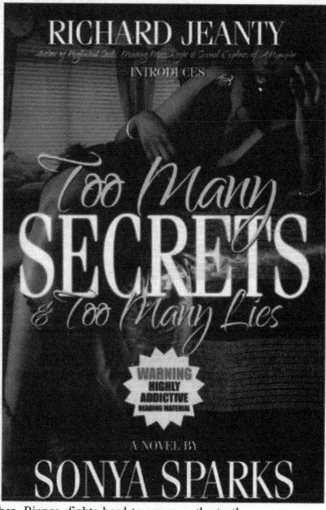

Ashland's mother, Bianca, fights hard to suppress the truth from her daughter because she doesn't want her to marry Jordan, the grandson of an ex-lover she loathes. Ashland soon finds out how cruel and vengeful her mother can be, but what price will Bianca pay for redemption?

**In stores!!**

RICHARD JEANTY

*Author of Hollywood Code, Daddy's Little Girl, and Ladies of a Nympho*

INTRODUCES

*Miami*

NOIRE

"The sequel to *Chasin' Satisfaction*"

WARNING
HIGHLY
ADDICTIVE
READING MATERIAL

A NOVEL BY

W.S. BURKETT

After Chasin' Satisfaction, Miko finds that satisfaction
is not all that it's cracked up to be. As a matter of
fact, it left nothing but death in its aftermath. Now
living the glamorous life in Miami while putting the
finishing touches on his hybrid condo hotel, Julian
realizes with newfound success he's now become the
hunted. Julian's success is threatened as someone
from his past vows revenge on him.

**Coming November 2008!!**

RJ PUBLICATIONS
INTRODUCES

Flippin The

# GAME

A Different Kind of Street Tale

a novel by
ALETHEA & MYLES RAMZEE

An ex-drug dealer finds himself in a bind after he's
caught by the Feds. He has to decide which is more
important, his family or his loyalty to the game. As he
fights hard to make a decision, those who helped him
to the top fear the worse from him. Will he get the
chance to tell the govt. whole story, or will someone
get to him before he becomes a snitch?

Evil Side of Money 22          Jeff Robertson

**Coming October 2008!!**

When an Ex-con finds himself destitute and in dire need of
the basic necessities after he's released from prison, he turns
to what he knows best, crime, but at what cost? Extortion,
murder and mayhem drives him back to the top, but will he
stay there?

**Coming November 2008!!**

Malcolm is a wealthy virgin who decides to conceal his wealth
From the world until he meets the right woman. His wealthy best friend, Dexter, hides his wealth from no one. Malcolm struggles to find love in an environment where vanity and materialism are rampant, while Dexter is getting more than enough of his share of women. Malcolm needs develop self-esteem and confidence to meet the right woman and Dexter's confidence is borderline arrogance.

Will bad boys like Dexter continue to take women for a ride?

Or will nice guys like Malcolm continue to finish last?

**In Stores!!!**

What happens when a woman's devotion to her fiancee is tested weeks before she gets married? What if her fiancee is just hiding behind the veil of ministry to deceive her? Find out as Sean Mitchell takes you on a journey you'll never forget into the lives of Angelica, Titus and Aurelius.

## In Stores!!

Use this coupon to order by mail

1.   Neglected Souls, Richard Jeanty $14.95
2.   Neglected No More, Richard Jeanty $14.95
3.   Sexual Exploits of Nympho, Richard Jeanty $14.95
4.   Meeting Ms. Right's Whip Appeal, Richard Jeanty $14.95
5.   Me and Mrs. Jones, K.M Thompson ($14.95) Available
6.   Chasin' Satisfaction, W.S Burkett ($14.95) Available
7.   Extreme Circumstances, Cereka Cook ($14.95) Available
8.   The Most Dangerous Gang In America, R. Jeanty $15.00
9.   Sexual Exploits of a Nympho II, Richard Jeanty $15.00
10.   Sexual Jeopardy, Richard Jeanty $14.95 Coming: 2/15/ 2008
11.   Too Many Secrets, Too Many Lies, Sonya Sparks $15.00
12.   Stick And Move, Shawn Black ($15.00) Coming 1/15/ 2008
13.   Evil Side Of Money, Jeff Robertson $15.00
14.   Cater To Her, W.S Burkett $15.00 Coming 3/30/ 2008
15.   Blood of my Brother, Zoe & Ysuf Woods $15.00
16.   Hoodfellas, Richard Jeanty $15.00 11/30/2008
17.   The Bedroom Bandit, Richard Jeanty $15.00 January 2009

Name_____

Address_____

City_____State_____Zip Code_____

Please send the novels that I have circled above.

Shipping and Handling $1.99
Total Number of Books_____
Total Amount Due_____

This offer is subject to change without notice.

Send check or money order (no cash or CODs) to:
RJ Publications
290 Dune Street
Far Rockaway, NY 11691

For more information please call 718-471-2926, or visit
www.rjpublications.com

Please allow 2-3 weeks for delivery.

PUBLICATIONS
BRINGING EXCITEMENT, FUN AND JOY TO READING

Use this coupon to order by mail

18.  Neglected Souls, Richard Jeanty $14.95
19.  Neglected No More, Richard Jeanty $14.95
20.  Sexual Exploits of Nympho, Richard Jeanty $14.95
21.  Meeting Ms. Right's Whip Appeal, Richard Jeanty $14.95
22.  Me and Mrs. Jones, K.M Thompson ($14.95) Available
23.  Chasin' Satisfaction, W.S Burkett ($14.95) Available
24.  Extreme Circumstances, Cereka Cook ($14.95) Available
25.  The Most Dangerous Gang In America, R. Jeanty $15.00
26.  Sexual Exploits of a Nympho II, Richard Jeanty $15.00
27.  Sexual Jeopardy, Richard Jeanty $14.95 Coming: 2/15/ 2008
28.  Too Many Secrets, Too Many Lies, Sonya Sparks $15.00
29.  Stick And Move, Shawn Black ($15.00) Coming 1/15/ 2008
30.  Evil Side Of Money, Jeff Robertson $15.00
31.  Cater To Her, W.S Burkett $15.00 Coming 3/30/ 2008
32.  Blood of my Brother, Zoe & Ysuf Woods $15.00
33.  Hoodfellas, Richard Jeanty $15.00 11/30/2008
34.  The Bedroom Bandit, Richard Jeanty $15.00 January 2009

Name_____
Address_____
City_____State_____Zip Code_____

Please send the novels that I have circled above.

Shipping and Handling $1.99
Total Number of Books_____
Total Amount Due_____

This offer is subject to change without notice.

Send check or money order (no cash or CODs) to:
RJ Publications
290 Dune Street
Far Rockaway, NY 11691

For more information please call 718-471-2926, or visit
www.rjpublications.com

Please allow 2-3 weeks for delivery.

# PUBLICATIONS
BRINGING EXCITEMENT, FUN AND JOY TO READING

Use this coupon to order by mail

35. Neglected Souls, Richard Jeanty $14.95
36. Neglected No More, Richard Jeanty $14.95
37. Sexual Exploits of Nympho, Richard Jeanty $14.95
38. Meeting Ms. Right's Whip Appeal, Richard Jeanty $14.95
39. Me and Mrs. Jones, K.M Thompson ($14.95) Available
40. Chasin' Satisfaction, W.S Burkett ($14.95) Available
41. Extreme Circumstances, Cereka Cook ($14.95) Available
42. The Most Dangerous Gang In America, R. Jeanty $15.00
43. Sexual Exploits of a Nympho II, Richard Jeanty $15.00
44. Sexual Jeopardy, Richard Jeanty $14.95 Coming: 2/15/ 2008
45. Too Many Secrets, Too Many Lies, Sonya Sparks $15.00
46. Stick And Move, Shawn Black ($15.00) Coming 1/15/ 2008
47. Evil Side Of Money, Jeff Robertson $15.00
48. Cater To Her, W.S Burkett $15.00 Coming 3/30/ 2008
49. Blood of my Brother, Zoe & Ysuf Woods $15.00
50. Hoodfellas, Richard Jeanty $15.00 11/30/2008
51. The Bedroom Bandit, Richard Jeanty $15.00 January 2009

Name_____
Address_____
City_____State_____Zip Code_____

Please send the novels that I have circled above.

Shipping and Handling $1.99
Total Number of Books_____
Total Amount Due_____

This offer is subject to change without notice.

Send check or money order (no cash or CODs) to:
RJ Publications
290 Dune Street
Far Rockaway, NY 11691

For more information please call 718-471-2926, or visit
www.rjpublications.com

Please allow 2-3 weeks for delivery.